THE SHIFTING PIER

The Shifting Pier

by

TREVOR WRIGHT

HAMISH HAMILTON · LONDON

HAMISH HAMILTON LTD

Published by the Penguin Group
27 Wrights Lane, London w8 5TZ, England
Viking Penguin Inc., 40 West 23rd Street, New York, New York 10010, USA
Penguin Books Australia Ltd, Ringwood, Victoria, Australia
Penguin Books Canada Ltd, 2801 John Street, Markham, Ontario, Canada L3R 1B4
Penguin Books (NZ) Ltd, 182–190 Wairau Road, Auckland 10, New Zealand

Penguin Books Ltd, Registered Offices: Harmondsworth, Middlesex, England

First published in Great Britain 1989 by
Hamish Hamilton Ltd

Copyright © 1989 by Trevor Wright

All rights reserved. Without limiting the rights under copyright reserved above, no part of this publication may be reproduced, stored in or introduced into a retrieval system or transmitted, in any form or by any means (electronic, mechanical, photocopying, recording or otherwise), without the prior written permission of both the copyright owner and the above publisher of this book.

British Library Cataloguing in Publication Data
Wright, Trevor
The shifting pier.
I. Title
823'.914[F]

ISBN 0-241-12603-7

Typeset in 11/13 Plantin by
Centracet, Cambridge

Printed and bound in Great Britain by
Richard Clay Ltd, Bungay, Suffolk

To Mandie

PART ONE

1

"I could have wept," Mrs. Jeffry said, but she didn't, she laughed instead; we all laughed. I suppose we always did the same as Mrs. Jeffry. When her faced dropped open into a smile, we all smiled too, beaming at each other like a group of light-bulbs set in a chandelier, glittering around her bedside. When she closed her eyes, we all went off into a sort of little seance, blinking surreptitiously around ourselves. We did it because we didn't like her, we didn't want her to notice us, we liked to remain a group, not to be singled out for a chat. We felt sorry for her, which was why we bothered; sorry because she'd been ill: more sorry still now that she was getting better. "I'll see another Christmas," she said, setting us worrying about presents for her, fretting about Christmas in the middle of August. The effect of dislike is hypnotic; in her presence we went into a sort of discreet hysteria; but there was no getting away.

We went up there for an hour every day, that August; the worst, wettest August anyone could remember, and so windy that the houses seemed to bend in it, touching the rowan trees, making quick new patterns on the skyline. I think she had an open fire in her bedroom, but I'm not sure; it might be that my imagination is colouring around the edges of the picture, blurred as they are now by time. We sat and listened – four of us, usually, unless Jenny had got out of it. She was the only girl, and good at getting out of things; it was her new talent, only to be surpassed later on by an emerging ability to get into things, instead. If she'd been lucky, she would creep up as we were preparing to leave, saying she'd been cooking, or dressmaking, or washing-up, but Mrs. Jeffry would be tired by then, and Jenny would apologise and sigh, as if burdened, though to this day I don't believe Jenny ever carried a burden in her life. Her eyes weren't made for it, just as her mouth seemed too perfect for conversation; her eyes were too beautiful for thought. On that day – the day when Mrs. Jeffry said she could have wept – Jenny was not about. The rest of us listened with the usual sense of vague resentment, the usual shifting unease. The old woman was talking about a film she had seen, many years before – she was too ill for the cinema now, though she had a television in her bedroom. "I could have wept," she said, talking about Norman Wisdom, the way he fell over. She seemed to admire the pathetic, she was developing it in herself, like a hobby; it was written into her movements, her language. "I'm a sick old woman," she used to say, beaming with the smugness of it, the satisfaction of illness, the complacency of disease. She told us how Norman Wisdom had fallen over a cat; the cat had run up a standard lamp; the lamp had fallen over onto a small drinks cabinet; a bottle of whisky had been knocked all over the trousers of Norman's girlfriend's pompous father. Norman had sung a song. Mrs. Jeffry could have wept. So could I, I think. With boredom.

At the end of the session, Jenny appeared on the stairs, panting becomingly, her hair artfully awry. "Oh, dear," she said as we came through the bedroom door. "I had to help Daddy." We all knew that she was lying; she knew we knew, but she said it anyway, her pretty eyes stiff with incompetent deceit. "She's asleep now, anyway," I said, watching Jenny place regret onto the front of her face and balance it there, like a juggling trick, and then drop it, waiting for the applause. I watched Jenny a lot; her neck fascinated me; it seemed a very erotic thing. She was fourteen, then; I was twelve or so; the others were my brothers, old men in their teens. "Come on, Tom," she said to me, for my brothers to hear, "let's walk down the avenue."

We walked slowly between the big rowans, tall, thin trees with the orange berries just starting to prick themselves out in odd clumps. The berries meant autumn, going home, going back to school, and a long winter without Jenny. I watched her long eyes, which seemed to turn the corners of her face, stretching to feline points above her cheeks. She liked being watched; we all did it, all three of us: we watched cousin Jenny as she slid carefully around the edges of our lives. Half-way down the avenue, half-way between Mrs. Jeffry's little house and our own holiday home, she sat down and lit a cigarette. She didn't offer me one, because she was selfish and didn't have many; it was one indulgence her father wouldn't finance. I didn't smoke, anyway, though in those days it was much more fashionable than it is now. A lot of things were safer, then.

She said, "How's the old bag, then?" puffing away maturely, blowing smoke. It fascinated me, the way she spoke: she had different languages; to this day, I have only ever had one. I never learnt the trick.

"Oh," I said. "She says she's getting better."

Jenny said, "Oh Christ," and looked straight up at the tree she was leaning on. I can remember the picture very clearly. Jenny looking up, showing me her neck; Jenny with something strong to lean on. "Where were you, today?" I asked, but she only looked severe and said, "I told you. Helping Daddy."

I sat beside her. "Richard's in love with you," I said. Richard was a brother. It was a family joke that the other brother should have been named Harry, but he wasn't. He was Phillip, but for some reason we called him Clem.

"Oh," she said, speculatively. "Richard."

"He told me," I said, which was a lie; I had overheard them talking about her; they did it often.

Jenny said, "It was Clem last time," which was true: they took it in turns to fall in love with her and then become infuriated by her. It must be a nuisance, being pretty, constantly disappointing people, failing to measure up. On the other hand, "But you love me all the time, don't you, Tom?" she laughed, and that was true as well, and we both laughed, as the wind wrapped up the rowan leaves above us,

11

the afternoon grew unseasonably dark, the tree roots we sat on were too cold for August. "Bloody weather," said Jenny, astonishingly, and stubbed out her cigarette-end on a pebble. "What are you going to do?" I asked her. "About Richard?": she only smiled, and said, "Leave it to me. Remember Toby?"

"Remember Toby" was her way of saying, "Jenny knows best." My father had bought me a dog, the summer before. He said it was to be called King; I wanted it to be called Toby, after a dog in some book I'd been reading. The petty dispute grew out of all proportion: my father wouldn't give way because he didn't understand how fervent this was in me; I wouldn't give way, because I did. The dog himself skulked in the house, not knowing what he had done to cause such quarrels; he started to mean nothing to me, the name began to mean more, as it can, with a child. It was Jenny, of course, who solved it. "Tell him his real name's King," she said to me. "And then give him a nickname. Lots of people have nicknames." So Toby lived on, and at last became popular, as a dog should be, and "Remember Toby" became a watchword between us, a little bit of intimacy. We were three brothers and we would each have given anything, those summers, for a bit of intimacy with cousin Jenny.

"Here's Uncle Roger," I said. Jenny's father was strolling towards us, down the rowan avenue, and Jenny hid the cigarette packet by stuffing it into my trouser pocket. "Hello, Daddy," she said, standing up, smiling, stretching her legs. I stood up too, feeling the packet in my pocket, blushing about that and other things. Uncle Roger said, "How is the old lady?" and Jenny replied easily, "Oh. She says she's getting better."

"Oh, good," her father said, and they strolled away together, his arm around her shoulders, Jenny saying shamelessly, "Yes, isn't it good news?" I was forgotten, but I had the cigarettes, incriminating but exciting, a guarantee of her return for them. It was nearly dark, dark before dinner, in August, in a summer that had everyone tutting, the sea neglected around the groynes while people stayed in their hotels and caravans and ate soup. I wandered off to the beach and watched a dog nosing the water, trying to catch it in its mouth. The water grumbled under the old, unsafe pier; I stood at the entrance, which was boarded up, with notices about danger and instability, though it didn't look any different from the past years, when we had wandered up and down it, kicking the abandoned, useless slot-machines.

On the night of my twenty-fifth birthday I lay in bed with Jenny beside me. My wife knew exactly what I was at; two hundred miles away, she ate alone, regarding my glum excuse, I imagine, with her usual tensile clarity. When Jenny turned away, I lit a cigarette. Jenny lay, her hair spread out like a map on the pillow, and said with a grimace, "Good God! You don't still smoke! Nobody smokes!"

I said, "I like that. It was you who started me on it."

She raised herself onto an elbow, and said, surprisingly, "Yes, I remember. You took to it very well. Like a good boy. Mind you, I didn't smoke then, you know. I just had them to impress you." She yawned and stretched, and my mind drifted back to that cold August summer, the summer when Jenny had kissed me, the summer when Mrs. Jeffry had died, even though the doctor had said she was getting better.

Richard and Clem were in my bedroom, giggling, when I got back. I felt they could see the cigarette packet, or guess that it was there, so I blushed again. They stopped giggling when I went in, and began treating me with their usual mixture of formality and dislike. They were fifteen and seventeen, a little laughing club of two, intimate, grinning, though they distrust each other now. "Ah, Tom," said Clem, and they began to ask me about cousin Jenny; she was their favourite game, the raison-d'etre of the club. "She'll be along later," I said, with bogus airiness, "for her cigs." I dropped them carelessly onto my bedside table. It was a draughty little room in a big, draughty house, a house full of uncounted rooms with holes in them. The ceiling was dripping in the rain, the drip singing like a little insect as it slid into a cocoa-tin put there by my father. The big house was Mrs. Jeffry's, but she didn't live in it, preferring her cosy hospitalisation in the little lodge down the avenue. So the big house was let to people like us in the summer, families that hadn't the sense or the money to go abroad for their holidays; because of our past connections with her, the old woman let it to us cheap. It was a great favour none of us wanted; we would sooner have stayed at home, but Mrs. Jeffry was the kind of woman you didn't offend. You did everything for her and remained always in her debt.

I was right: Jenny came along quite soon, and she had changed from her jeans into a perfectly white dress. It was energy she had, clarity rather than elegance: at fourteen, she wasn't even tall, but she shone with confidence. Clem and Richard stared at her, and she said to me, "We'll go for a walk after dinner, if the rain stops." I was twelve; she did it to excite the brothers; it was obvious, but it worked.

I was excited during dinner – family dinner, all of us there, the brothers, me, our father, Jenny, and her parents; the two families shared the house. Jenny's mother was an awful cook; she seemed sad all the time, her eyes following people about with a desperate sort of randomness; the food she cooked us on holiday seemed sad, too. I was agitated by thoughts of an actual walk in the dark: Jenny sat, predictably demure, sipping brown windsor, crunching lettuce: it was always salad, even though we were damp and shivering. Uncle Roger watched Jenny more than he watched his wife: I felt I couldn't blame him for that. My father looked confused, as usual. They said he'd been confused since Mother died, but I wouldn't know: I was too young when it happened to remember anything, though of course I knew that that was when Mrs. Jeffry had stepped in, and looked after us children, with her hidden, benign cruelty, thus leaving the whole lot of us in her debt for ever more. I try not to think of the woman like this, but I can't help it, even though I of all of them have particular reason to be grateful to her.

The rain stopped, but it remained ridiculously dark. Jenny and I set off in wellingtons across the empty field which lay between the house and the beach; she held my hand because of the slippery mud; we wore anoraks. She walked with her usual purposefulness: this was no aimless ramble. She delivered me to the pier gate; she leant against a danger sign and gave me a cigarette. I lit it in silence, though I didn't want it: the rules were clear, if the game was obscure. There was a strong wind, sending invisible spray in hard bucketfuls across our faces, creaking the makeshift barrier across the entrance; you could hear the whole pier shifting along the length of it, further out than you could see, swinging slowly around a deep axis. It had given way, the previous autumn: a girl had been standing where the hole came; she had drowned. I didn't know much about it; I wasn't adventurous; I hadn't found out if it was a small, girl-sized hole or one much bigger: you couldn't tell from the beach, even in daylight, though you could see that the pier was adrift, moving sinuously, waving slowly, like a rope.

Jenny removed the cigarette from my mouth, which was no particular relief, since I had just discovered that I liked smoking, and then she kissed me. I liked that, too. It seemed expert; indeed, I felt expert myself, she made me feel practised, though it was the first time I'd ever kissed anybody, except for my mother, long ago. It lasted a very long time, then finished abruptly; my mouth tasted of somebody else, for the first time in my life.

"That," said Jenny, "was a reward for walking the pier for me."

I said, stupidly, "But I haven't walked the pier," and Jenny replied, obviously, "No. But you're going to."

I turned and tried to look down its length, but it disappeared quickly: you could only guess which way it was leaning. We'd all been warned about the pier; I was as frightened of recriminations as I was of the hole, the sea, the cold. I never fancied the sea much, even as a child. Others ran at it screaming, begging it to attack, flinging themselves in and out of it in expert abandon, but I always hung back, reluctant to yield myself. Now she wanted me to teeter twenty feet above it, lurching like a tightrope walker, with only the black water to soften the long fall. "No," I said. "I can't do that."

"Oh, but you must," she said, with no persuasion in her voice at all; just certainty. "It's your half of the bargain." That was Jenny, and still is: making bargains single-handed, holding people to them with her long fingers. "You've had your kiss," she said, pretending to be petulant, so I moved one of the wooden horizontal planks aside, levered it until the nails worked out, hinged myself through the gap, felt suddenly confident because the wooden floor was unexpectedly firm. "All the way," she said. "Bring me a toffee-apple." I spread my arms, like a sleep-walker, and set off.

All the time I could hear the sea, feel it underneath me, feel the pier reacting to it, one minute resisting its movement, the next minute succumbing to it. I found the handrail at the edge and again felt confidence, surging like the sea: I held the rail like a ballet dancer, creeping unashamedly, already out of sight of land and Jenny. I kept my weight always on my back foot until my front foot secured itself, testing for emptiness, step by step. It was incredibly dark; there were no shore lights and no moon: the weather was too poor for either. Exhilaration began; the silence, the dare and, of course, the kiss. I lifted my head; there was no point in looking down; I couldn't see the floor. I began to strut, like an actor, the wooden pier my own stage, the scene my own particular tour-de-force. I was about to declaim into the wind, when suddenly my right foot found no ground and my left hand lost the handrail.

There was a pain the length of my shins: I was sliding down into darkness; then I was sitting, my legs dangling. I was on an edge; the sea was below me, uncovered; I had found the hole. I could feel my pulse, up in my neck; lights danced at the back of my eyes; my breath was louder than the wind. I coughed and sat, beginning to wonder what to do next, frightened to move.

I didn't know how far along I'd come. I sat there, while it started to rain, framing me all round with water. Then I started to edge sideways along the hole, still sitting, moving into the centre of the pier, lifting myself along on my hands and bottom. Once, I thought I heard Jenny calling: perhaps I'd been a long time; I had no idea. Each time I moved, bits of wood splintered their ways down, hitting the noisy water in silence. I thought I must have traversed the full width of the pier when my right leg butted up onto something; I'd come to the end of the hole; there was a narrow stretch of pier running past it; I supposed I had to continue. She hadn't been joking about the toffee-apple: there was a stall full of them at the far end, and it was a joke in the town that they were all still there, the owner not daring to rescue them. I thought of my father worrying, and wondered if it was late; I couldn't have seen a watch, even if I'd been wearing one. I crawled sideways until I found the handrail on the other edge; then, I pulled myself up and, huddling the edge, I began to press on.

There were shapes in the darkness. They frightened me, but it was a rational fear. I didn't believe in ghosts, at that time; I didn't consider that there was an after-life and the shapes, which were chewing-gum machines and machines that gave you a gift every time, worried me because they were positioned along the handrail; I had to step out and around them, towards where the hole might have been, if it extended that far. I clutched each machine as I wormed around it. I hugged one so hard that it shifted abruptly from its brackets, sending me staggering backwards towards the void; I was numb with fear, but I banged hard into something solid, something upright, some sort of wall, and I leant against it, panting, relieved. Relieved because I knew then that I was at the end of the pier, leaning against its only building, a decrepit amusement hall with a toffee-apple kiosk.

She stuck the toffee-apple into her pocket, hardly looking at it, or me. I had hoped for another kiss, but none came. Everything was business-like; the contract had been fulfilled. We strode together back to the house; she demanded my hand for the slippery bits. We weren't, in fact, very late in, but my father looked puzzled at our entrance, and Uncle Roger put his arm round Jenny, as if claiming her back from me.

★ ★ ★

I was in my pyjamas when she came into my room, still dressed. She said, "You're a good boy, Thomas," and kissed me. Then she said, "You can tell Richard he can take me to the pictures tomorrow." I didn't know what to think, or say: I said, "O.K." and she went. I put the light out and sat in my chair, in the dark, listening to the rain on the skylight and in the cocoa-tin. My mind was moving like the sea at night. I suppose that I sat there for about five minutes, before Mrs. Jeffry said to me, quite clearly in the darkness, "Well, what happens now?"

Despite what anyone has said about it, I was not asleep or dreaming. Mrs. Jeffry said, "What happens now?" and, astonished to hear the bed-ridden voice, I jumped up and put on the light. She was not there, of course. My room was empty, save for me and my expansive confusion, and Mrs. Jeffry was at home, upstairs, in bed, and quite dead.

2

What I do remember about my mother's death, which happened when I was six, was the beginning of a new face for my father. He never looked the same again, even when he was happy, which of course he was, eventually, occasionally. I think he was perplexed more than anything else; he seemed never to understand the point of it; nor, increasingly, of anything much. We were on holiday, in the big house, when it happened: it was a road accident, a shopping expedition, a lorry. The house changed too; changed its smell; it was then that I noticed the water leaking in through the roof, though I was rather young for symbolism. I know my father cried, though I didn't see it; it was a big enough house to hide in, and there was always the rowan avenue, where you could see anyone coming two hundred yards away, and compose yourself. My brothers cried, too, openly, and it was at that time that they started to look strangely at me, wondering what was the matter, why I seemed unaffected. Because I was not surprised when my mother died, when she was late back from the shops, when a police car turned up instead. The doctor said I was sublimating; it would all come out, eventually, a great flood of it; but it didn't. After a while, Clem asked me why.

"I don't know," I said. I wanted to help him; he had never shown so much interest in me: I was flattered. But I really didn't know. It wasn't that I wasn't unhappy; I was. The point was that I seemed to have expected it; as it were, to have known about it in advance.

Anyway, that was when old Mrs. Jeffry – old even then –

strutted up from the little house and, without asking anyone, began to take over, washing us, feeding us, putting us to bed. I don't think my father liked it, at first. He used to follow her about the house, turning his puzzled stare from her to us and, if she was there, to Aunt Joyce, Jenny's mother. She was no help. She had enough trouble, coping with her one daughter; she was one of life's spectators; she seemed absent even when she was there. I remember Mrs. Jeffry sitting in the bathroom, watching me as I bathed. "I'm the best you're going to do," she used to say, with grim satisfaction. "I know I'm not your lovely mother, but I'm all you've got." When my father protested, saying she was doing too much, it was too good of her, she used to tell him, "I like children, Mr. Fellows." I was only six years old, but I knew she was a liar.

We stayed in the big house much longer than usual, well after the end of the holidays; I suppose my father couldn't face going home alone. Mrs. Jeffry told us how to treat him, explained to us what he was feeling; she seemed to think she knew him better than us: we all grew to hate her. After a week or two she started smacking me from time to time, saying things like, "Your mother should have given you a bit of this. It'll do you good." She was always talking about Mother; increasingly, she criticised the way we'd been brought up – though never in front of Father, of course. She could make Richard or Clem cry any time, grumbling about Mother, her mouth folded with criticism, screwed up like a paperclip; but I wouldn't react; it became a matter of pride. I suppose that that was why she hit me, not the others.

What Mrs. Jeffry did like was television. I think she thought she was in a play, with us: no, not a play: a soap opera. She thought we were sharing an episode of *Coronation Street* together; she watched it three times a week, drawing her attitudes, her understanding of things from it.

Anyway, we went home eventually, back to Birmingham, and Mrs. Jeffry came with us. She wasn't ill then, of course; she had a strange, rigid sprightliness; she seemed made up of sticks. At Christmas we went to Uncle Roger's; Mrs. Jeffry came too – to look after us.

Jenny was eight, then, archly able in games and in parent management. She was having a record player for Christmas – not a toy one, a proper one, the size of a small suitcase, sitting, wrapped, under the tree. "That's a Dansette," she said to me boastfully; I had no idea what she was talking about. "It's got 33 and 45," she added, sitting on the arm of the big, adult chair I'd been allocated, swinging her legs. "It's got a red top." I remember that when she opened the parcel, next day, her eyes grew wide with astonishment. "Daddy!" she cried, and there was arm-flinging and rapture, while Aunt Joyce looked sadly around. I think they actually believed that they had surprised her, failing to notice that she had specified model, make and colour. Well, that was Jenny. She has a most elaborate hi-fi system nowadays, of course, received, I imagine, in similar circumstances – though not from her father.

They all went in for a salad supper, on Christmas night. Aunt Joyce had managed a turkey roast, but she reverted to salad at the earliest possible moment. The sitting-room was left deserted except for me; I had been forgotten, which was a nuisance, since I hadn't indulged at lunch, and I was hungry. I sat and looked round the empty room, littered with curls of empty wrapping-paper, and I wondered what to do. It would be rude not to turn up at dinner in Uncle Roger's house; on the other hand, perhaps it would be more rude to go in late. Mrs. Jeffry was very keen on rudeness: it was a corporal offence. I waited to be called: nothing happened; I felt more and more hungry; if it went too far, I might get hiccups, another sin in Mrs. Jeffry's eyes. I could hear the faint sounds of mealtime down the passage, the clicks and laughs: no-one seemed to be remembering me. Nothing good could come out of it, I knew even then, though I was only six, full of vague panic. In the end I made for the Christmas tree, crawling beneath it: I was looking for one of the chocolate decorations, though in fact I didn't much like chocolate. I couldn't think of anything else to do.

I was sitting there, half-hidden in the greenery, the chocolate ball more or less unwrapped, when Mrs. Jeffry came in.

She had finally remembered me, she was looking for me: I knew that for some reason it would be bad if she found me now. I sat very still indeed, holding my breath, very frightened, very guilty of something. Then for some reason the tree lights went off, and she looked hard my way, and then she was screaming at me about rudeness, deceit, gluttony, thievery, moving at me as she shouted. Her hand went under my arm, she screamed and screamed, she hauled me partially upright and hit my ear, which was already red with shame. She hit me a second time, in the same place; my ear was hot, my head somehow awry, my eyes, of course, swimming. Her hand went up again; I could see no end to this; but then there was another voice screaming, a smaller, faster body coming at us, some sort of tussle in front of me.

"Get off him!" she screamed. "Get off him, you old bag! He's just hungry! What's it to you? Who do you think you are? Get off him!" Then my father was there, and Uncle Roger, pulling Jenny off Mrs. Jeffry, who shook with rage as well as physical shock, and eventually Aunt Joyce came in and looked dejected.

It didn't make much difference. My father didn't banish the old woman; she herself didn't repent and stop hitting me; even Jenny showed no particular signs of increased friendliness, afterwards. But in some way, I was changed; in a sense, it was as though my reserve had been broken. I saw that things didn't have to be as they had become; that, in fact, things as they had become were not as they should be, the old woman lording it about my life, obtruding over mealtimes and bedtimes; things could and should be different. I cried for the loss of my mother, that night, for the first time since she had gone, six months before.

We piled into the car, next day, to go home. For some reason, I used to sit in the front seat, in Mother's place; Jenny leaned in through the window and said, very audibly, "You watch that one. She's after your father." I still wonder if she was right about that. I can't see that Father had much to offer. Mrs. Jeffry wasn't poor, by any means: I can't imagine that Father was particularly attractive. She sat in the back, with Richard and Clem; there was a great fuss about getting home in time for a Boxing-Day edition of *Coronation Street* – she had her own room in the Birmingham house. I saw her that night, through her open door, in silent homage before the television, her back to me, her head bowed.

Six years later, on the night of my first kiss, she said to me, "Well, what happens now?", lying dead as a plank in a different house. It frightened me, the concreteness of the voice, the clear, physical presence of it, the unspirituality of it, in the dark air of my bedroom. I checked the time: eleven-thirty; I opened my door, to check that she wasn't actually there, on the landing, but of course she wasn't; she hadn't been out of bed for two months. It didn't keep me awake, though; too much had happened that evening for my mind to rest on any one thing; it drifted, in a circular fashion, lulling me to sleep like a carousel, or rocking me, like a cradle. Next morning, all was solemnity at breakfast: for the second time in six years, there was a death in the family, though our reactions were different now. Our problem was to conceal our relief; Clem and Richard managed quite well, discussing practical matters with Father, arrangements; Jenny barely tried, saying things like "Good job, too," semi-audibly. For me, it was different, because, once more, I seemed unsurprised. After breakfast, Jenny took me down the rowan avenue, stopping me half-way down it, looking quizzical. "You're funny," she said. "You're a funny one." She gave me a cigarette, without smoking herself, she stared at me, leaning on a tree. Jenny always leaned: there was always something, or someone, available to be leaned on. "You knew about this, didn't you?"

I had already decided not to tell anyone about the voice, which I had heard, evidently, after the old woman's death. But Jenny was a great waiver of decisions, a great unmaker of minds: she crumpled resolutions like bedsheets. I said, "She spoke to me, last night," knowing that Jenny at least wouldn't say I'd been dreaming, I'd been agitated by sex and jealousy, I'd been personifying my guilt. They were all possibilities, of course; I'd already run through them; but nothing could explain the simple, physical fact of the voice. Jenny seemed to believe that.

"That's weird," she said. "Christ!" We sat down, she pulled me down, I smoked, she talked about seances, ouija boards; she knew a bit about everything, did Jenny, enough to get along. She asked me if it had ever happened before; I didn't think it had. She asked me if I wanted to do anything about it; I didn't think I did. The conversation drifted to the welcome demise of Mrs. Jeffry; I was just beginning to realise what wonderful news it was; and I was just beginning to feel guilty about thinking that. "God!" said Jenny. "Remember that Christmas?"

I'd never forgotten it. We talked about it, lying on our backs, side by side, looking up at the sun, which was putting in a rare appearance. You could look straight up the length of the tree; there was a long stretch of bare trunk craning like a neck below the high branches; and there were more berries every day, glinting like little bulbs. "Good God," said Jenny. "It's sunny."

We lay there, quiet. The air was thick as soup with flying creatures of every description – gnats, mosquitoes, ladybirds, flies, wasps, craneflies, bees, butterflies. Jenny said, "It looks like the Battle of Britain up there." Things kept landing on her; she smacked herself hard, complaining; it reminded me of Mrs. Jeffry, the sound of irritable little slaps. "Good God!" Jenny said. "What's going on?"

I tried to explain to her that the rarity of sunny weather was to blame. "These things are all lying dormant," I said. "In a normal summer, they'd come out a few at a time. What you're seeing is probably a month's worth of insects in one day." She turned her head and looked along the ground at me. "Really?" she said, smiling; I didn't know why. After a long while, she said, sleepily, "Mmm. That sounds nice."

I said, "What does?"

"Lying dormant," she said.

* * *

Richard took her to the pictures, and she found me later in the big sitting-room, and told me about the film. After a time, she said, "Listen, Tom. I've been thinking." Richard or Clem would have made a joke, but I just said, "Oh?"

"Tom," she said. "What did she mean?"

I said, "What?"

"'What happens now?' What do you think she meant, Tom?"

It seemed so obvious to me that I hadn't given it much thought. On the other hand, I didn't much want to explain to Jenny that hers was my first kiss, my first infatuation, that Mrs. Jeffry had been voicing my own confusions as to what happened next, what I should do about it. So I said, "I don't know. I mean, I haven't really thought about it."

We were sitting side by side in a window seat, our backs to a big, Victorian window, looking across the shabby, panelled room, which for some reason contained a large billiard table. No-one else was about. "Well," Jenny said. "I reckon she said it as she died, Tom. She died just before eleven-thirty." We sat and thought about that; the eyes turning in, the slight choke, the shudder into immobility. "I reckon she was saying, you know, what happens next? After you've snuffed it? What then?"

I said, "Oh. I'd never thought of that." It was true: I'd assumed that the question was directed at me; a reproof for my recklessness, on and off the pier. I thought about it now. "Well," I said, after a while. "What does happen next? When you've snuffed it? What does? What do you think, Jen?"

She looked serious, just for a moment. "I don't know," she said, with more circumspection in her voice than I'd ever heard. Then she brightened up. "Well, never mind," she said. "I expect you'll find out, soon."

I said, "Soon? What do you mean?"

She grinned at me. "I expect she'll tell you," she said.

3

I thought that house was so big. I thought it had rooms you couldn't count, a lake in the garden. I thought that it was separated from the sea by a field. It seemed possible to disappear into it, to cultivate solitude, to skulk in attics, worrying that no-one had noticed. I think the rowan avenue added to the effect: a long, military arrangement, aloof, austere, guarding the flat landscape from very little. The storms evolved themselves quite comfortably above the rowans; the winds found their way beneath the high-starting branches. I thought there were about two hundred of them.

I counted them, yesterday: there are thirty. The house has four bedrooms – big ones, admittedly – and an attic; there is a small pond. A small area of scrubland stands between the house and the sea; I had thought it a long walk, once, holding Jenny's hand; a long walk, but not long enough. The scale of things has changed as I've grown up; they have got smaller, though no easier; I have got bigger, in some ways. The pier, of course, has gone.

Sex with my wife is like a mutual, or joint, investigation. Although I am thirty-five, I seem to be learning the ropes – even though we are hardly just married. It is delightful, in some ways, but so unlike my occasional night with Jenny when, unaccountably, I seem to become an expert. Not that Jenny is easy to impress: she is an experienced girl, and older than me. I slept with her two weeks ago and, for various reasons, I told her that I thought my wife suspicious of us. "Yes," said Jenny. "Well. I expect she would be."

I was smoking, as usual on such occasions. I sat on the edge of the bed, listening to the London traffic. "Well," I said. "Ought I to stop seeing you?"

It was raining outside, the thin whine of city rain, the sleaze beneath the tyres. Jenny was stroking her own throat in small, distracted movements. Her eyes held mine for a few, lazy seconds, and then she began the slow, winding movement which would eventually bring her to sit up, to get up, to drop her nightie to the floor, to require, perhaps, to be bathed. "Oh, yes," she said, "you definitely ought," and we both thought about the impossibility of that.

On the morning after Mrs. Jeffry's death, before my walk with Jenny, I had a chat with my father. He called me into a little-used downstairs room which I thought of as the library, though it had no books in it. It was a place for serious talks.

My father sat at a desk; it was a very formal business. He said, "Mrs. Jeffry. Well. Now. What did you think about her?"

I didn't want to tell him that I hated her vehemently, that she hit me when he wasn't there, that she grumbled about Mother, that she knew nothing except what happened in *Coronation Street*. As usual, therefore, I said nothing at all.

He looked hard at me, looking puzzled, but concerned; interested, as it were by some small, unimposing phenomenon, such as a butterfly in an odd place. "Well?" he said. I wondered what this was all about – though I had my suspicions.

"She was all right," I said.

"Ah," said Father. "Oh. All right."

I said, "Yes." I was trying to be polite without telling lies: I was following Mrs. Jeffry's precepts: she insisted on courtesy and honesty, though she herself showed neither.

"Well," said Father, "she seems to have been very fond of you." It was a preposterous remark; I couldn't see how anyone who had lived in the same house as us could have possibly made it; but I didn't want to argue, and, besides, I wanted to get away. Jenny had promised me a walk, and I was still remembering the taste of her, last night.

I said, "Oh. Good," and Father sighed and said, "All right. Off you go." He didn't explain it at all, but by then I had realised what he was talking about, anyway. The old woman had left me everything she owned, including the house we sat in. Her will had been left very obviously in her bedroom, on top of the television. She had told me about it herself, that morning, after breakfast, as I sat alone in my bedroom.

All week, nobody mentioned the will. I began to wonder if I'd imagined it; I was quite prepared to believe that, to write it off, all this posthumous conversation. She'd said "What happens now?" but I might have been having an emotional nightmare: then she'd told me about her will, the next morning, when I was still half-asleep. It was easy, and highly desirable, to rationalise the thing away, despite Jenny's support. After all, she only believed it because it made a better story, it passed the wet summer away; and I hadn't told her about the will, about the morning chat with Mrs. Jeffry. That was too easy to verify; I thought I'd wait until somebody mentioned a legacy, which they'd have to do, eventually. It was a sort of test. So I went for a walk with Jenny, who said, "You knew about this, didn't you?" and I waited out the days until the funeral.

She was going to be cremated, on a Thursday morning. I was looking forward to it; I was a curious youth, and I had never seen a cremation. More to the point, I suppose that I was hoping that the actual physical disintegration of Mrs. Jeffry would put a stop to her attempts at communication with me; it wasn't logical, but then of course talking to ghosts isn't a logical business – especially when you don't believe in them, or in God, or in anything except beginnings, middles and ends. The brothers and I were in the second car: we were the closest she had to a family; we, and the cast of *Coronation Street*. Jenny was in another car: this was one occasion she couldn't wriggle her pretty way out of. The vicar started some mechanical intoning. He was quite clever, telling us what a fine woman Mrs. Jeffry had been, even though he'd never heard of her before that bleak Thursday morning. You could just hear the pause as he inserted her name into the blank spaces of his little paean: he had another one to do, after all, in twenty minutes.

I didn't believe in any of this, as I've said, and anyway I hated Mrs. Jeffry with all the bitterness of puberty, so I spent my time looking round the chapel. It was terrifyingly cheerful. Neat, municipal flower arrangements kept their appointed places on the scrubbed, white walls; the plate at the altar had been well duraglitted; it looked nearly gold. The windows were small, for a church, but some had geometric little attempts at pictures: souls nipping up to heaven, relieved to get away, smiling down, travelling first class with their clothes still on. I imagined Mrs. Jeffry doing that: her coffin bursting open in the fire, which I could hear through the trap-door; Mrs. Jeffry climbing out in her Crimplene trouser suit, pushing off from the coffin-lid like a swimmer at the baths; sidling upwards, flying like an apprentice superman. I caught Jenny's eye, in a different row; she grinned, and winked. I watched her as she picked up a prayer book. For some reason, and quite openly, she tore off a page of it, as if it were a memo-pad. I watched fascinated – fascinated as usual – as she wrote something on the page, and handed it back to someone in my row, nodding towards me. It was like passing notes in class, except that it was quite unfurtive. It read: "This is a corpse-processing plant."

She was right. I suppose that even the bereaved might find some subliminal consolation in a real church, with its background rhythm of birth and marriage as well as death. This place was a mere monotone, and I looked up from the note to see the doors opening and the coffin sliding away on its conveyor belt. This factory was automated.

Anyway, that was it. We all stood up and sang a hymn, or rather mimed it to a recorded, enthusiastic choir, the air swelling with the ardour of nobody at all. Behind us, in the doorway, the next party was already gathering: did they have the coffin with them? Had they leant it up against the wall for a rest? We passed them as we left, feeling, I suppose, rather embarrassed: none of us was grieving; Jenny was singing. The vicar might have looked nonplussed, if he'd thought about it. I looked back to see him jotting something down on his service sheet. Presumably, he was erasing Mrs. Jeffry's name, putting in the next one, filling in the cracks.

A man – one of the undertakers – whispered at me. "Would you like to see the flowers?" Apparently it was all part of the ritual, if you can call it that. A little pile of wreaths, most of them in plastic bags, had been deposited in a corner of the asphalt car-park. We all had to stand round them, looking at them: perhaps we were checking on the quality, or quantity: after all, we'd paid for most of them. We stood in a solemn little line, actually saying things like, "That's a nice one," and "Look at those fuchsias!" I had a brother either side; Father was behind me, Jenny in front. Father put his hand on my shoulder; he still hadn't told me that I was the old woman's heir, that I was rich, that, at twelve, I owned two houses. Well, I thought. Perhaps I don't. It didn't occur to me at that stage not to trust Father.

Jenny was in front of me, in a new black coat; her shoulders were moving, her hair bouncing on her neck. I realised that she was laughing, silently, convulsively: the shudders were spreading in a quiet, little quake. In a second, she would laugh out loud – she had a very noisy laugh, like a crow – but fortunately, or perhaps deliberately, Father said then, "Come on, we'd best be off home," so the family started folding itself back into the big, musty hire cars. Jenny said, "Uncle David, I'd rather walk, if you don't mind." She gave the impression of being upset, assuming an expression of distant suffering, of perceived torture. I don't know if Father was fooled; he wasn't as besotted with her as her own father was, but he said anyway, "Yes. Oh, I see. Well, Tom had better walk with you, then. We'll see you later."

We watched the cars roll off, and Jenny started laughing again, and then I started too. I have never laughed so much, before or since, though I don't know what we were laughing at. Jenny kept saying "Would you like to see the flowers?"

and I kept saying, "Oh, yes, they're awfully good value," and we had to hold each other up. The next party came out, and wandered over to their little floral heap. We were incorrigible, completely out of control, watching these mourners glancing nervously and confusedly at this glum selection from the florists. Then Jenny grabbed my arm, and pointed upwards. At the top of the long, industrial chimney was the beginning of some smoke. It grew, like a swarm of bees, climbing up into the air in a thin line. "Oh, my God!" screamed Jenny, literally hysterical with mirth; several strangers glared at us and muttered. "Oh, my God! There she blows!"

I was laughing so much that I could hardly see: my eyes were full of tears. Above us, Mrs. Jeffry wafted, presently to settle on flowers, to be breathed in by people and dogs, generally to add to the pollution of the seaside atmosphere, just as she had done in life. We sat down in the car-park, we lay down, helpless; I watched the spiral of smoke, comparing it in my mind with the stained-glass images of resurrection: was that smoke Mrs. Jeffry's black soul? Eventually, we got to our feet, and began walking, passing the vicar as we dried our eyes. Perhaps he was glad that somebody had managed to cry for her after all.

For a while, it seemed really possible that I wasn't going to hear from her again. I dreamed a lot; the nights were like swimming through dark water, full of strange, contradictory tides, frightening little whirlpools; they were harder work than the days, which were suddenly long, easy and empty. All the fear had gone, the fear which had really begun one Christmas, six years before, the fear which had been Mrs. Jeffry yelling, "Elbow-grease is what you need, there. Didn't your lovely mother tell you about that?" Her face twisted round a cruel little pivot, creasing with delight, her mouth full of spite, her smile stretched out for Father. "I do my best for them," she used to say to him. "Of course, it isn't much."

There was a sense of loss, of tension suddenly unsprung; not only no more fear, but no more lying to Father about her, no more defending her, which we used to do, for some reason. "Don't go crying to your Daddy, he's got enough on his plate," she used to say: and we didn't. We covered up for her, we kept quiet, we said she was all right.

I woke one morning from a difficult dream, a dream in which I'd been inside an egg, a massive egg buried under the ground, fashioned out of white bricks. I sat at the bottom of the egg, twenty feet from its top, quite unable to escape, to climb up the smooth sides to the exit, which was a door, up at the top. I tried to crawl up; I slipped down. The whole thing was like a fable; nothing about it was unexpected, but it was very vivid: the impervious, dry bricks, the particular, rounded quality of the echo. It disturbed me a good deal; I told Jenny about it: she laughed at me.

I was annoyed. "So, what's funny?" I asked. We were in her bedroom, for once, the bedroom of someone converting herself into a grown-up – a dressing-table, perfume, a Cliff Richard poster.

"Oh, come on, Thomas," she said, bouncing on the edge of her bed. "Trapped in an egg? It's got to be symbolic."

I wasn't stupid; I knew what symbolism was; I was clever at school. I could see her point, too: eggs were Freudian, all right. I said, "Am I trying to escape from the womb?" and we started to laugh again, and she said, "Whose womb? Not mine!" I laughed, though in fact I had only the vaguest idea of what a womb was; they didn't tell you at school, in those days. Anyway, my egg-dream was not symbolic: I was sure of that. "Oh, well, please yourself," said Jenny, dismissing me. She was going out with Richard; she had to get to the dressing-table.

But it made me angry to be laughed at, so, soon, I told her about the will, about my message from dead Mrs. Jeffry concerning my legacy, even though I had no proof about it at all. She said, "Golly, we're all going to be rich! I hope you remember me, afterwards," and she flounced off out, to a dance-hall, I think, with some girlfriend she'd made in the town. I didn't know what to do. I went out into the garden and lay down. It was about seven o'clock, still light, of course, in late August; warm, too, for once. I watched the sloping, evening, autumn light, modelling each blade of grass separately, from the side. The big house, ugly though it was, looked golden; each brick cast a shadow onto its neighbour; the walls seemed to ripple. Crab-apples were falling early; they lay around the tree, the centre-piece of the lawn. Each fruit was a startling, rich red, very small – too small to be of any use. Mrs. Jeffry had always made me collect them, or pick them, if she was early enough: she used to say that pork wasn't pork without crab-apple jelly. I don't know why she said it; she certainly never made any; after a week or so she would say that she'd never had the time, and I would have to throw them onto the compost-heap. No doubt crab-apples were a byword of some character from the world of soap-opera.

It was particularly pleasing to be able to lie on the grass there at the back of the house and look at the crab-apples and know that I was not going to have to do anything about them at all. They could sit there, and get eaten by birds, and inhabited by late wasps, and rot and compost themselves, without my help. For a minute or two, I felt just like one of them myself: suddenly left alone to get on with it. After years of stricture, rotting seemed a warm and comfortable prospect. But then I started to worry about Jenny again, to fill with sexual jealousy, to wonder why she laughed at me sometimes, when laughing with me was so much more fun. The two years between us seemed a complete generation, sometimes; she seemed to have lived a complete, self-contained life before she'd even met me.

And then there was Mrs. Jeffry, and the question of whether I was going mad. It was quite a possibility. Any intelligent twelve-year-old spends a good deal of his time, probably most of it, wondering whether he is going mad. It doesn't help to be the possible subject of spiritual interest by a nasty, dead old woman. It seemed to me then that it was time to find out something, to prove something, to myself, of course, but also to Jenny. I didn't want her laughing at me any more.

★ ★ ★

It was dark when I came out of the back door, that same night, just past twelve o'clock. I stepped across that same lawn, feeling the little apples under my feet: I was wearing slippers. It wasn't the best way round to the rowan avenue, but it was possible, and it was quiet. I had to climb through the garden hedge, which proved altogether more difficult and painful than I'd imagined; the spikes pulled at my clothes, taking off one slipper, sliding inside my pyjama jacket, tickling my shoulders. But then I was on the dirt track that ran between the tall trees, and I simply had to follow it. It wasn't too dark; not as dark as the night of the pier walk; there was a decent moon, casting a shadow. It was very cold indeed; colder than we were used to, even that summer: there could almost have been a frost. I made no sound as I moved; partly, that was why I was wearing slippers.

It took about two minutes to walk the length of the avenue, which was a private track whose sole function was to link Mrs. Jeffry's two houses. I don't know why I wanted to go back to the dead woman's home; I don't know what I expected to find there. I suppose that I was going to look in her bedroom, on the television-set, in an effort to find the will – at twelve, you don't know much about legal process. I don't know either what I was playing at, wandering about in the middle of the night: I could presumably have gone there any time. But I did think that there might be where I would find an answer.

I should add that by an answer I mean something concrete – if not the will itself, then some notes, a letter; I don't know. I am not trying to suggest that I was being lured there by some supernatural urge. It would be easy to put it that way, now, but as a child, I was too rational for that approach. I think that in a sense what I wanted proof of was not that the will existed, but that it didn't.

The police were keeping an eye on the empty house; I suppose that meant that a Panda car passed the end of the avenue once a day. They certainly weren't about, then; it was very easy to get in; burglar alarms were not the vogue then that they are now. It was pretty isolated, out there; doors were often left open; not many strangers passed. As I think I've said before, a lot of things were safer, then.

Mrs. Jeffry's door wasn't actually open, but a window near it yielded easily. I got my body half in; at full stretch. I could reach back round to the front door, and release the latch from the inside. That hurt my stomach: I rested a bit, felt a bit sick. Then I went in.

The electricity was still connected, but I felt I had to be selective in my use of lights: I didn't want anyone to spot me. She had a small sitting-room, which I lit with a table-lamp. I didn't expect to find much there; she hadn't lived downstairs for over two months. It was tidy and dusty, a room full of gaps, where photographs, ornaments, mementoes had been removed, taken upstairs, like Mrs. Jeffry herself. There were even rectangles on the wall indicating missing pictures. It looked a bit like the scene of a robbery, and it made me suddenly furtive, shamefaced. I switched the lamp off, knowing that the bedroom was the place to look.

I hadn't seen the old woman dead. I'd been tentatively invited to, to see her "lying in state": but that was one state I didn't want to see her in. So I hadn't been to the bedroom since our last joint visit, when she'd talked about Norman Wisdom in an old film, and told us that she was getting better. Then she'd had a stroke.

I put the bedside lamp on, and then quickly drew the curtains. Even empty, the room was claustrophobic; it seemed full of ghosts, but I don't mean the ghosts of Mrs. Jeffry and her new, dead consorts. I mean the ghosts of all the dead conversations, the tediums; I could hear her voice, droning on about *Crossroads*. I could remember her, looking craftily at me, obviously wishing she was fit enough to start hitting me again. I felt uneasy, but not because she was dead; rather, because she'd once been alive.

There was nothing on top of the television. If there had been a will there, it would have been taken away a week ago; that was obvious. Beside the set was the *TV Times*, still open at the day of her death, with some serial episodes marked in biro; she'd drawn boxes round them, framing them like the photographs that filled her room, which was exactly as overcrowded with stuff as her downstairs was not. I picked up the papers, realising how little I had seen of this room, even though we had spent hour after hour there, during her illness, told by our parents that we felt sorry for her, listening to her drivel. All that time, I'd been thinking of somewhere else, of getting outside, of Jenny. I'd stared at the junk without seeing it. There were loads of it; especially, there were lots of very old photographs, oval, Victorian-looking things, faded round the edges, faded, indeed, in the middles: packed with grey grain.

A few days later, Jenny said, "Well. Go on, then. What colour are the walls, at school? In the dormitory?"

I'd been sleeping there for over a year, but I couldn't tell her; she'd proved a point. I had looked at those old pictures, sometimes with apparent intentness, avoiding the old woman's gaze. Now I saw that I'd no idea of what they were about, no idea at all. They weren't interesting; old family scenes: she must have had a family, once. She must have been a child. But whatever they were, I'd stared at them for hours, and never seen.

Well, I suppose that was a moderately interesting thought, at the time, but it didn't help. I picked up the papers, as I say, realising all the time what a stupid errand I had involved myself in. Beside her bed were some novels: not romances, as might have been expected, but crime novels, some of them, to my twelve-year-old mind, quite racy in appearance. There was nothing under her bed, except a lot of sticky dust, which might have been spiders – I was frightened of spiders: spiders, not ghosts. There were some miscellaneous medicines in her bedside drawer; I couldn't tell what they were for; as far as I knew, she'd had everything wrong with her. There were also bits of entirely mystifying apparatus: red tubes like octopuses, with squeeze-bulbs; and there were pieces of jewellery. Nowhere else was there any kind of container that could have held papers, a copy of the supposed will; there were just a lot of artefacts.

So, that was that. I put the lamp out, and turned on my torch, flashing it once more around the room, throwing odd objects into sudden, meaningless relief; a last, random look about. I'd left the room and started across the landing before something made me turn back – something I'd seen had made a belated impression. My torch found it; for some reason, I didn't put the light back on. I trod carefully across the thick carpet – it was a comfortable room, warm as an oven – to examine it more closely.

It was a photograph; a very old one indeed, in a gilded frame with the gilt coming off it; one of the oval ones. Indeed, it was the oval shape that was the first attraction.

Mrs. Jeffry's face was strung tightly onto bones; it wouldn't have changed in seventy years. The forehead was flat, overhanging the furious little eyes; the mouth twisted, unless stretched deliberately into a smile. I saw the face in the photograph: a girl of five or six, a little character at the beginning of a journey that was to end one Thursday in a seaside crematorium. The face was unmistakable.

But it wasn't the face, or the white swaddling lace, that interested me, it was the setting. It was an unusual picture, an early flash print; the artificial light was ricocheting around. The child was seen from a small distance, and from above, her face raised to the photographer. The angle of shot foreshortened the little body, revealing a fair amount of the surroundings. The little girl was sitting, quite clearly, at the bottom of what could only be described as the interior of an enormous, smooth egg.

I watched that picture for some time, wondering whether to take it away with me, to show it to Jenny and ask what she thought about symbolism now. I sat there in the dark, the spot of my torch on this old snap of my dream, a picture of a place I seemed to know for no apparent reason, and I must say that, despite my rationalism, the hairs on my neck found a little insect-like life of their own. It was a very quiet night, although it would be fanciful to suggest that, as I sat there on the edge of the bed, I could hear owls hooting. I did hear something, though; something much more normal, and so much more terrifying. In a room below me, I heard the distinct sound of an ordinary, human cough.

I got downstairs, using the torch. I was, in all honesty, very frightened; on the other hand, I found myself unable just to run for it. To leave without trying to find out what was going on seemed simply impossible; after all, I had come there to find some answers. Perhaps I also thought that Jenny would be proud of me if I stayed; I don't know. What I did was to make my way in the dark, the torch off, sliding along the wall of the small downstairs lobby, towards the only room I hadn't looked in.

It was the kitchen. If there was somebody in the house – and I was still thinking in terms of body, not thing – it had to be in the kitchen. Nobody had come in after me, I was sure of that; and acoustically, it would be from the kitchen that one would hear something while in the bedroom. There wasn't a light anywhere, and I think I was very quiet, in my slippers; I don't know if I was expected; I don't think so. I opened the kitchen door, then flicked on my torch, then flicked it off again and left the house as quickly as I could.

We had raced the rowan avenue many times, the brothers and I. It was a natural running-track, straight as a Roman road. The brothers had always won, of course. They worked together, and were older than me. But they wouldn't have beaten me that night. My legs shifted like a wheel; my neck swivelled like an owl's as I watched for pursuit. I was sick, this time, when I got home. I made a lot of noise in the bathroom; only later did I realise how fortunate it was that I'd disturbed no-one in the house.

I had seen a face in Mrs. Jeffry's kitchen. It wasn't a photograph, it wasn't an illusion, it certainly wasn't a spirit. I was as sure of that then as I am now, over twenty years later. The face was moving slightly, in the beginnings of recognition: I had turned off the torch very quickly, but the face was familiar, despite the odd shading and angles thrown up by the torch, the unnaturally sinister arching above the eyes. It belonged, of course, to Mrs. Jeffry.

4

Mrs. Jeffry was ill for a long time. It seemed to make her more evil – perhaps she was in pain – but less powerful. Her face grew tauter with disease, unnaturally young; her eyes found a sort of feverish enthusiasm.

I remember those eyes, gleaming; she was looking at some photographs that she'd laid out on the kitchen table, in the Birmingham house. This would be about 1960; I was ten. Her visits were already decreasing, though she still had her own room. Travelling was becoming difficult for her.

"Come and look at these, Tom," she said. They were pictures I didn't remember having seen before; they were all of my mother. She was pushing a toddler – probably me – on a swing; she was standing by a big, Ford car; she was marrying Father. These photos had been hidden away, I suppose, at her death; but the old woman had found them and set them out for me, like playing-cards in a game she was still determined to win.

It was pointless, really. Even an emotional child would find it difficult to cry after four years. I took an interest instead, commenting on the composition of the pictures, on their content. I had a little camera myself; I was interested in photography.

It was about then that I realised she was taking to the bottle. That same evening, she called me from her room, as I passed the open door. She stank – of sherry, I think it was; her eyes were fixed on me with the stare of the drunk who has to concentrate even to look straight at you. The television was on: the news.

She said, "Sit down, Thomas, boy." I'd never been in that room before; I'd looked in; the door was always open, so she could keep an eye on things; we used to creep past it. It was odd, seeing a bit of your own house converted into somebody else's, a sort of no-go area in a familiar land.

I sat near her, as indicated, on a little pouffe. It made me feel low and awkward; it was not the sort of furniture we had, elsewhere. Her mouth was wet, though I couldn't actually see a bottle, or a glass.

"You think," she said carefully, "that I'm a wicked old cow, don't you, Thomas?"

I wasn't surprised by the language. As I understood it, Mrs. Jeffry was rich, but she was the most common person I'd ever met. She was the exact reverse of the rest of us: we were poor, but snobbish. Anyway, I'd heard Jenny use far worse terms than that one – usually in connection with the old woman herself.

What did surprise me, of course, was the sudden honesty and directness of approach. I suppose that was the drink.

Anyway, I didn't know what to say; but that didn't matter. I'd been invited in to listen to a monologue.

"You're right," she said, slowly. "You're right, boy. I'm a nasty, old, woman." She watched the news for a time, then the weather forecast. It was going to rain; she tutted, and said, "They're never right."

I said, "I must be going to bed, Mrs. Jeffry," and I stood up, but she said, "Just you wait, Thomas. Just you wait."

I didn't know what she meant. I sat down again. I was then, and still am, eager to please anybody. Increasingly, it seems a flaw in my character.

"You wait," said the old woman, screwing up her eyes. "I'll see you right, Thomas, boy. One day, you'll see. I'll put you right. I'll put you in the picture. Won't you be surprised?"

I didn't give it a second thought. A ten-year-old doesn't have much time for the drunken ramblings of an appalling old woman. But it was an extraordinary interview and, obviously, I didn't forget it.

★ ★ ★

A week after the funeral, when we were packing up to go back home, I asked my father if there'd been a will. I was trying to be casual, not looking at him. He was emptying a cupboard in the big sitting-room, the cupboard where we kept plastic tennis-racquets, a croquet set. They hadn't been out since we'd got there, a month before. It hadn't been a summer for it, what with the weather, and the old woman dying. The billiard table had been well used. I was leaning on the edge of it now, watching Father's back, which seemed to stiffen.

He said, "A will? You mean Mrs. Jeffry? Why?"

He might have just wondered what a twelve-year-old wanted with a will, but it seemed a suspicious response to me then. "I don't know," I said. "I just thought people left wills."

"Oh," he said. "Yes, they do. But it's a complicated business, you see, Tom. It's a drawn-out business." He coughed and put the racquets into a dustbin liner, and went out. He was a stranger to me, then, as always: a distant, preoccupied man; but I had always thought him fair, straightforward. I didn't like the way his back bent as he left the room; I didn't like the time it seemed to take him to load the bag into the car. It was disturbing, suddenly to find myself wondering about him. It wasn't an emotional disturbance – as I say, he was always a stranger to me; it was as if a respected public figure, or a basic law of nature, like gravity, had been called into question. It made me think of Mrs. Jeffry's dead voice. The universe was expanding: if Father could be a liar, then anything, including spiritual chat with a dead, detested enemy, was possible.

There were a couple of days left of that difficult, eventful holiday. I felt depressed, though I'd survived the awful weather, the holiday disappointments – and, of course, the old woman's death – without depression. I left Father to the packing, and wandered out of the big house, climbing up the little mound that stood by the lake. At the top was a bricked-up entrance to an air-raid shelter: a brick arch, built into the raised ground. I used to sit there, looking down at the lake, when I wanted to be alone; I wanted to be alone now, to work on the readjustment of the world necessitated by the notion that parents could tell lies, keep things to themselves. It was a worse discovery than the other one I'd made, six years before – which had been, of course, that they could die.

Anyway, I was to be foiled. When I got to the top, I found Auntie Joyce, Jenny's mother, standing, looking down at the water. I said, "Oh. Hello," then felt embarrassed, because I'd sounded disappointed to see her; and because I'd never been alone with her before, and didn't know what to say. She always seemed to need cheering up.

She said, "Hello, Tom." For a time, it seemed that that was to be the conversation in its entirety. I sat down on the grass; she stood beside me. Then I said, for no reason, "Where's Jenny?" She looked at me for a long time. She was either thinking deeply, or not at all: nothing in between. "Oh, Tom," she said. "I don't know."

That was the way she spoke. Anyone who didn't know her would assume that Jenny had run away, or committed suicide, but Aunt Joyce could make a recipe for meat pie sound tragic. I mean that seriously; I'm not being facetious; I have heard her in the kitchen, working with Jenny, mentioning quantities of flour, teaspoonsful of black pepper, sighing wanly. I don't think anything awful had ever actually happened to her. Perhaps that's worse; perhaps you just fret about what it's going to turn out to be; at least Father had had his share, had got it over with.

Anyway, we both looked down at the lake, thinking our different thoughts, and after a while I said, "I suppose parents tell the truth, don't they? To children? Do you think?"

She breathed for a time. "Oh, Tom," she said. Then she sat down beside me, and we carried on looking at the same thing – a pond, a lake. "What a question," she added, unemphatically. "Don't you know?"

I didn't. I didn't know many adults at all. I listed them in my head. No mother. Ambiguous father. And teachers, of course. At boarding school, all other forms of adult company were banned, anyway. Even parents were banned, most of the time. So the only adults I could claim to know in any sense at all were my teachers – and they, like all teachers, were habitual liars. It didn't look too promising.

"Oh, I don't know," I said. "I mean, I thought I knew, but I don't know now."

"Well," said Aunt Joyce, and I thought she was smiling, "there's a story." There were some ripples on the lake. Either there were fish, or it was starting to rain. Aunt Joyce said, "Jenny smokes cigarettes."

I didn't know why she'd said it. I said, eventually, "Oh, does she?" and she replied, "Didn't you know?" and I said, "No."

Another pause; some more ripples. I could see the tops of the rowans, beyond the house, jam-packed with red berries.

"There you are," said Aunt Joyce. "You know perfectly well that Jenny has cigarettes. Why tell me you don't know? That's a lie isn't it?"

I was embarrassed again – I was getting used to it. "I'm sorry," I said. "I meant no harm."

She looked at me, and I noticed that she was beautiful. She had Jenny's cat-like eyes, but her face was fuller, more generous. It was a revelation; I had never seen beyond her habitual misery. "Jenny lies to us about smoking," she said. "We lie to her about not knowing. Nobody means any harm."

I could see the point. My eyes suddenly opened on a world in which everybody was at it, in which lying wasn't an isolated, specialised activity, but the general currency among ordinary, decent people. I was learning too much, that summer. The ground, as they say, was being swept from under me: I was on a pier, instead; a shifting, anchorless pier, moving with the sea.

There was a stranger in the kitchen, but I didn't pay him any attention. The house had been full of strangers, that week – solicitors, undertakers, even a reporter from the local paper. I was preoccupied by the fact that the world was growing as I watched it, with the fact that I was in love all of a sudden with a woman of thirty-five. The man was speaking to Father, who looked shiftily at me. Both men were sitting at the big, wooden kitchen table. They stopped talking, when I went in; Father looked as though he were making a decision; finally, he made it. "Tom," he said. "I want you to meet Mr. O'Cleary."

The stranger turned to face me. He was a broad, handsome man, pleasant-looking, smiling, oddly interested in me. At first, I was frightened. He didn't seem startled, however; he showed no recognition; he nodded happily when I said, "Hello, Mr. O'Cleary"; he said, "Pleased to meet you, Tom," in a rich, Irish voice, and seemed to mean it.

Well, there was no reason why he should know me. We had met before, of course; I recognised him straight away, although on our previous encounter I had had only the briefest look at him. He, presumably, had not actually seen my face at all. It had been behind a torch-beam, a beam which had been shining directly into his eyes, two weeks ago, in Mrs. Jeffry's kitchen.

What was extraordinary was that a face could so resemble Mrs. Jeffry's and yet appear sunny, benign, attractive. I suppose he looked how the old woman would have looked if she'd had any aspect of pleasantness in her character. Perhaps a face isn't either handsome or ugly; perhaps that depends on the light behind it.

It was Mrs. Jeffry's face, all right. Not only in the sense that it looked like her, but in the sense that she had created it; made and bequeathed it. For, as Father now explained, Mr. O'Cleary was Mrs. Jeffry's son.

I didn't know where he'd come from. Mrs. Jeffry must have been married, once, I supposed; after all, she was called "missus". On the other hand, she was also called "Jeffry": why didn't her son share the name with her? They certainly weren't going to tell me; the air was stiff with embarrassment, Father's embarrassment, despite Mr. O'Cleary's cheeriness. I was to be introduced, that was all; they had something important to discuss; I was to play with Jenny. Well, that was fine. I wanted someone to talk to. A problem had presented itself. I wasn't stupid, as I've said before. I knew why long-lost sons suddenly turned up from Ireland when rich old women died. It happened all the time, on television.

Which was a clue, of course.

There were two trees on the back lawn: the crab, which stood like a china ornament, right at the centre, and a willow, twenty yards away, at one end. I made for the crab, and sat at its base, picking up the fallen apples, and tasting them. They were quite soft; some were sweet, others sharp; I bit into them, one at a time, throwing them half-eaten onto the grass. I was thinking about Mr. O'Cleary.

I wasn't alone on the lawn, though it took some minutes for me to realise it. The willow-branches formed a massive, conical tent in the summer; when I'd been younger, I'd played hiding games in there. Someone was doing that now. I chewed an apple, and leant against my tree trunk, and watched.

There were two people under there, and they didn't know I was watching them. Jenny had her back to me. She was standing, her feet slightly apart, her back slightly arched. She was kissing someone. There were arms around her neck.

At twenty yards I could only guess how passionate it all was. It was certainly enduring; in my case, painfully long. I don't know why I felt so cheated. I knew she entertained the brothers in this way, in turn, as it were; it made the summer bearable for us all, provided a focus for our energies and curiosities. I suppose the problem was that I hadn't actually seen her at it before; that, and the fact that I now considered myself to be in contention. Anyway, I watched the kiss for what seemed like a number of minutes; I watched the arms snaking about, I cried, I felt like a spy. They did stop, eventually; they did come out from the willow, hand-in-hand: Jenny and Clem.

They didn't seem to see me; I was grateful for that. They wandered off laughing, into the kitchen – where, presumably, they were greeted by the disturbing sight of Mr. O'Cleary. I didn't want to see any of them; I went to bed, thinking how relieved I'd be when term began again, the dormitory with its comfortable dirty jokes.

She started on at me as soon as I reached my bedroom. By moving around, I could hear her more or less clearly; it was like positioning a transistor to get the best signal. "They're up to something," she hissed, a noise like static, breaking in the evening air, in front of my face. "I've told you, Thomas, boy, that's all for you. It's all yours. You're going to lose it, boy. Get a shift on. You're going to lose the lot."

I was standing right by the door – it was the best signal. "Mrs. Jeffry," I said, "what's going on?"

She carried on. She might have been answering my question; she might not. I didn't know if this were two-way communication; or one-way, for that matter. "You watch them," she said. Her voice had only ever had about three tones. This was the most common one, the spiteful, spitting one. "You watch your father. You're going to lose the lot."

That was the end of that. My flesh didn't creep, the temperature didn't drop, my table-lamp didn't rise into the air and then smash violently to the floor. Mind you, it wouldn't have proven anything if it had: I might have done it myself.

Jenny came in. She never knocked; I suppose she worked on the basis that she was always welcome – anyone she chose to visit ought to be grateful. Well, in my case, she was right.

"God!" she said. "Have you seen him? The playboy of the western world?"

We talked about Mr. O'Cleary. "He's here for the money," said Jenny; and then, remembering something, "Hey! I thought the old ghost had promised it to you!" I said nothing; I didn't know whether I was being laughed at. "You'd better watch it," she said. "He's muscling in on your millions."

I said, "I saw you kissing Clem."

"Yes," she said, smiling. "He's absolutely hopeless."

"But I thought it was Richard, at the moment."

She didn't answer: it was none of my business. "What about that face!" she said, talking about the Irishman, sitting herself down on my bed.

I said, "You know that dream, Jenny? About the egg? Do you remember that? Well, I've seen it." I was determined to

46

prove something. "I've seen it," I repeated, as she was paying me no attention at all, smiling in at herself.

"What?" she said.

"I've seen the big egg," I said. "It's in a picture, an old photograph. In her bedroom. She's sitting at the bottom of it. Where I was, in the dream, actually." She still seemed unimpressed, so I added. "I broke into her house. The other week."

She looked carefully at me, at last. "Hang on," she said. "You're saying that there's a picture of this egg thing, there, in her room?"

"Yes."

"Where, exactly?"

"Oh. On the window ledge, on the same wall as the bedhead."

She seemed pleased. "There you are, then," she said. "That's where your dream came from. You've stared at this picture hour after hour, pretending not to be looking out of the window. That's it. You've stared at it without ever seeing it. It's all subconscious."

"Oh," I said. I hadn't thought of it; I had more or less assumed, since seeing the photograph, that the egg-dream had been another message from the old woman. I think I felt relieved – and, possibly, disappointed as well.

Jenny stood up. She had sorted me out, again; now she was off. "You going to bed?" she said. "It's a bit early."

I said, angrily, "Yes I am."

"Oh," she said. "Right." She opened the door, then turned, and added, "By the way, you shouldn't wander about in here talking to yourself, you know. You sound completely bonkers from outside." And then she was gone.

5

Mr. O'Cleary asked me, "Where does a fella go to get a drink in this God-forsaken town?" His eyes were twinkling, as usual; his voice chattered like a stream in a field. He was a parody of himself, at times; a parody of the Irishman, all charm, melody and brogue.

Nevertheless, it was a ridiculous question to ask me. I was twelve years old; I had never visited a public house in my life; we drank wine at Christmas. As for Newport, the town where, in a sense, I lived, I was almost entirely ignorant of it. Downlanders were allowed to walk through the High Street only on certain occasions, and always with prior permission. You could be caned for entering a shop, never mind a pub; anyway, you were always in uniform. I was once beaten very severely by a prefect – a lad, as I now realise, of about seventeen – for taking off my cap in town. That was Downlands: a boarding school of the very worst type – insignificant, dowdy, envious of its prestigious competitors, and run almost entirely by a cabal of brutalised teenagers. My father paid out a substantial sum, a good deal more than he could afford, to obtain for me this privilege.

Nevertheless, I was glad to be back. It was a detestable place but I had some friends there; and there were no girls, no petulant cousins, no sadly beautiful aunts. I sighed with relief on the first day as I stacked my locker in my new dormitory, hiding bits of tuck that wouldn't last long, finding a science-fiction novel, a surprise from Father, at the bottom of my case. I snorted at that, and slung it onto the lower shelf: Father was a liar. I usually cried a bit before going back, more out of politeness than anything else; this term I hadn't bothered. It was good to be at school: at least we all worked to the same rules.

Well, things settled as they do in such institutions; everybody quickly forgot that there was life outside, other ways of being; and then, on the first weekend, as we were lining up for rugby trials or some such purgatory, Mr. O'Cleary appeared in the large foyer of Aston Hall, which was the junior boarding house, and informed me that we were going out for the day. I was panic-stricken; as I've said, contact with the outside world was strictly forbidden – and here was this big, startling man explaining to Matron that I'd be back at tea-time, that he was an old friend of the family, that she wasn't to worry. Well, Matron was as lonely as the rest of us. She didn't have a chance.

We careered off, out of the town, climbing constantly, gradually, in Mr. O'Cleary's Morris Traveller. It was a filthy car, particularly inside; it seemed that he had been carrying earth in it, or manure; I began to feel sick, and to panic. However, it wasn't long before we emerged from the corridor of trees into the harsh, autumn sunshine, at the top of a hill.

It was Detford Ridge, a local beauty-spot. I'd never seen it, but I'd heard of it: it was where older boys claimed they took local girls on Sunday afternoons; at that time, I believed them. We climbed out of the car, and wandered to the edge, Mr. O'Cleary saying, "Well. Look at that, now!" We were standing on a small lump of limestone, stretching its way out of the grass like a bone; below us was a vast, rural landscape; I suppose that we could see for forty miles, in a straight line. It was, I suppose, beautiful; I didn't appreciate that kind of thing then, though I would now. Although now, I expect, the National Trust will have installed its litter-bins.

"That's a lovely house, where you spend your holidays," he said, conversationally, sitting down, producing some sandwiches from a cardboard box. "My mother's house, I mean," he added.

I sat beside him, leaning against a bit of rock, watching his eyes, which seemed to be enjoying everything; he seemed even to find the process of opening a paper-bag slightly, gently amusing. "Yes," I said. "Mr. O'Cleary, have you come to England about the will?" There seemed no point in not mentioning it; why else had he come to see me at school? My father never did.

"Oh, no, no," he said, as if I'd made a joke. "No. We don't want to bother about that."

"Oh," I said. "Oh. All right."

He said, "What did you think of her, then? The old woman?"

It reminded me of my father asking the same question, though it could not have been more differently done. I chewed a bit, on a meat-paste sandwich; I liked meat paste. "She was very kind," I said. "She did a lot for us."

"Oh," he said. "Oh. I see." He took a peach from the box, and threw it at me; I caught it; we were playing, now, two strangers on the verge of a contract. "Only I had the impression myself that she was the most fearful old baggage." He was opening a bottle of beer, using a metal opener; there were no cans, then. Then he was giving the bottle to me. I was shocked; not so much by being invited to drink beer, but by being invited to do it without a glass. I had some, anyway; I took to it immediately – like kissing Jenny.

I said, "But she was your mother . . ."

"Ah," he said. "But I never knew her, you see. You see, I'm a bastard."

I said, "Oh, no, you're not!" I didn't know him but I couldn't see any reason for such a description; he was the only man I'd ever met who smiled all the time. I would have swapped him for my father, at that time, like a shot.

"She gave me away," he went on, stretching, leaning back on the obtruding rock. "She got rid of me at a very early age." He didn't seem to mind, so I leant back too, and looked out across Detford Ridge. We were sitting there on a cliff, looking at mile upon mile of seabed, seabed consisting now of field stacked on field, submarine farmhouses, giant, crusty oaks, like corals. I said, "Bowls," and he laughed loudly. "What?" he said. "Oh, yes. The bowls. You think you're on Plymouth

Hoe, do you?" He was right; we had been doing Francis Drake at school; I was watching a tiny hay lorry, weaving and tacking round the lanes, tracing its way across the panorama, and I was thinking of Spanish galleons. I suppose I was fairly drunk.

"Now then," he said. "It's a few million years since that lot was an ocean." It was swimming, though; at least, it seemed so to me. I was dozing off; I heard him say again, "We're not going to worry about that"; then I was waking. "Come on," he said. "Better keep Matron happy, hadn't we?"

I slouched in the filthy car beside him, and said, "What about the giant egg, then? What about that?" He simply drove on. Even though I was drunk, for the first time in my life, I knew that I wasn't making sense. I tried to shut up, to watch the road through the front window; I was feeling sick again.

As we drove into the town, I said, "But, listen, if she gave you away, how did you know? How did you know she'd died? You must have found out. How did you find out?"

He took the car through the main gates, the gates that the boys weren't allowed to use. "What?" he said. "Oh. Oh. I see." The car stopped outside the main door; we weren't allowed to use that, either; nor the huge oak staircase; these things were for the parents, who paid for them. Matron was standing in the doorway; she looked as though she'd been waiting for me. "Well," said Mr. O'Cleary. "I'm sure you've noticed. I mean, you must have noticed, with the old woman. She has this way of getting through to you, doesn't she? If you know what I mean."

I said, "No. What? I don't know . . ." and then Matron opened the door of the car, and said, "Come on, now, Thomas," which was ominous in itself: Christian names were only used when you were in trouble. I said, desperately, "Mr. O'Cleary. Do you mean . . .?" and Mr. O'Cleary said, "Oh, that's all right, call me Tom," which was my name, and I said, "Did she talk to you, do you mean . . .?" and Matron said, "Mr. Althorpe wants to see you," and hauled me out of the car. Some boys were watching and grinning from the common-room window. The car pulled away. Matron lead me inside. Once again I was guilty of something or other.

Jenny was laughing uproariously, flinging herself about on my bed, hysterical in a way that made me envious; I was remembering lying beside her in a car-park, unfolding layer after layer of hilarity. Now she was on her own again; again, she was laughing at me. "Christ, Tom," she said. "You're twelve years old, aren't you? What the hell did you ask him that for?"

Richard came in, then – looking for Jenny; she was often in my room; one way or another, I made her laugh. "Oh, Richard," she said. "Tom asked Mr. Althorpe what a bastard was!" Richard started laughing, too; soon he would tell Clem; the house would be ringing like a distant opera. "Well," I said. "I didn't know." It seems incredible, now, but it was true: at the age of twelve, I didn't know what the word meant – except as a playground term of abuse. These things simply weren't explained, in those days. My house-master had quizzed me about O'Cleary; he wasn't pleased about my outing; it was typical teacher tactics to blame me for it when the guilty adult was safely out of the way. We had sat in his study, which was full of red leather; he had a slight twitch in his cheek; it caught and clicked about, especially when he was angry. I watched it as he spoke to me, leaning in towards me, then moving back, trying to be magisterial. I didn't trust any of them.

"You know, Fellows, that we don't – ah – like the idea of – ah – our boys going out for the day. We do like, you know, a little notice. At least." Nobody was frightened of Althorpe in the personal sense. He was known as Faceache. I watched him, the cheek curling in and out of the face, sucking up to the bone, then dropping away. I suppose he could see me watching. I said, "Sir, what's a bastard?" I was still suffering from half a bottle of beer; and, I suppose, I wanted to shock him; after all, I knew it was a dirty word.

Anyway, he didn't tell me, of course. I have always found that the last thing teachers seem to want to do is actually to impart any useful information. My father had to be telephoned; I had to be suspended from school, which unfortunately meant nothing more dramatic than spending three days in the empty sick-bay. Then I was allowed back into what they called "school life" without, as far as I can recall, signing any confession or experiencing a show-trial in morning assembly. After that the term jogged on in its normal fashion; Christmas came; we went to Uncle Roger's, as usual, and I told Jenny about my indiscretion in a misguided attempt to impress her.

"Anyway," she said, "I knew he was. I mean, look at him. He had to be a bastard."

Richard said, "Of course he is. She had him when she was very young – she's Irish herself. I think she was a servant, or something. Anyway, she got rid of him pretty quick, one way or another. Later on, she married this Jeffry, who died before we knew her. No other children." He was being informative, sitting down on my bed, next to Jenny; he was trying to impress us with his adult knowledge.

"Has she been in touch, at all?" Jenny asked me suddenly. I was crimson, immediately; burning with anger; this was a confidence. Richard looked at us both, and said, "What? Who?" I watched Jenny very carefully; I thought, as I think now, that I was about to find out a lot about her. She smiled her arch, feline smile; she allowed her hair to move on her head. "Oh," she said. "Oh. Nothing."

I was so relieved, I wanted to kiss her – though, I suppose, that was hardly unusual. She had shown me danger, and held me back from it; I felt only grateful. Richard went, and I found myself babbling, thanking her for not embarrassing me. "Come here," she said, and I sat beside her, and she did kiss me, a full-length kiss, as it were: a kiss involving shoulders. "I won't hurt you, Tom," she said, although of course she did, every day, every time I saw her. "Thank you," I said.

After a while, she said, "What about it, though? The old bag? Has she been at it, really, though?"

I trusted her; I don't know why; I don't think I was much of a judge. "Oh, yes," I said, truthfully. "Oh, yes. Just about once a day."

6

It had started in the sick-bay, where I was supposed to be living out my disgrace. You went up some stairs and then down some again, for no apparent reason, in the way that you do, sometimes, in converted houses. You climbed over this little hump in the corridor, and you were in sick-bay, where Matron lived, though there was nothing sick about her. She was young, pretty and, I think, divorced; occasionally, men used to visit. All the boys loved her, one way or another. There was nothing wrong with being in sick-bay.

Except, of course, that I was there in shame; not sick at all. It was a small wooden room with three beds, white drawers. I was shown in and told I'd be let out in good time. I didn't care; I'd brought Father's science-fiction novel; I was missing physics, which I particularly hated; Matron seemed sorry for me. After all, it was she who had permitted the jaunt in the first place.

She started on at me the very first night – Mrs. Jeffry, I mean, the voice breaking in the air, spitting like static. It hadn't happened since the time on holiday when Jenny had overheard and mocked me for it; I'd thought it was over; at that time, I found it easy to forget about the voice in between visitations. "Now look," she said. I was sitting on the bed; lights-out was organised leniently in sick-bay. "Look at the trouble. He's got you into trouble already! You're going to lose the lot, if you're not careful. I've already told you. You've got to watch that one. He means you no good at all!"

I spoke out loud, as I always did, to no avail. Matron was

in her sitting-room; she had a visitor; I could hear two sorts of laughter. "Listen," I said. "Mrs. Jeffry. Is that you?"

"What about it, then?" she said, or, rather, screamed; "What about this, then? They're making a complete fool of you, boy. That's your lovely father for you, if you want to know."

I said, "I know, I know. All right . . ."

"Up the garden path," she said; I could practically feel her breath on my face; I remembered smelling it, the bile, the sherry, when she'd been alive. I said, "She'll hear you!" and she said, "Nobody hears me, boy. You watch the lot of them. They're all liars. You watch that cousin of yours. She's a little bitch, as well . . ."

I dreamed all night. I was held, fast; I was in the giant egg again, climbing towards the top, sliding down; Jenny was looking down through a door, laughing; a six-year-old Mrs. Jeffry was crawling beside me, tugging at me, crying, her flat little face twisted. She was shouting, "Dolly! I want Dolly!" and grabbing at me, yelling, "Where's Mummy now? Where's our lovely Mummy now, then?" I wanted to hit her in the face, but I couldn't: you don't hit little girls, not even evil little ghosts of girls, not even in dreams. I watched them both: Jenny, up at the top, with me prostrate, yearning towards her; Mrs. Jeffry below, clinging, with more strength than a child is entitled to, screwing her face up, forcing her lips into little ridges; a six-year-old face with a small moustache. I looked from one to the other, the one laughing, the other screaming; and I realised, as I sweated and struggled, my fingernails bursting on the bricks, that they were both the same.

Matron said, "That was quite a night you had. You don't need to worry so much, you know. Worse things have happened."

I said, "There's a dead old woman who talks to me at night. I hate it. I hate her. It's something to do with an egg."

They say that madness is political: if enough people think you're mad then, by definition, you are. I don't know about that, but I do know that my nervous breakdown, as it's become known, began its long fermentation at that moment, when that young, pretty, conscientious, empty woman looked at me in a way that suggested that insanity, or at least delusion, was a possibility. I suppose that you're mad if you imagine that you talk to dead people; at that moment, over breakfast in sick-bay, it occurred to me that if you aren't imagining it – if you really do talk to ghosts – then you're probably just as mad, anyway. Or, quite possibly, madder.

I had the same look from Jenny, that Christmas, in her father's house, when she asked me if I'd heard from the old woman. "Oh, yes," I said. "Just about once a day." I couldn't blame her. I was known in the family as a non-believer, a down-to-earth lad, full of common sense. There was nothing mystical about me. "Look," she said. "I think you really mean this."

"Yes," I said. "Of course I bloody mean it." She was more shocked by the language, coming from me, than by the conversation itself.

"In that case," she said, "I really think you ought to talk to somebody. I mean, I thought it was a joke, at first. Or a dream, or something. It's not right, you know. Thinking things like that . . ."

I said, "I can hardly think about anything else. She comes on every night. She says awful things, Jen. About Dad, and O'Cleary. And you."

"Really," she said; her voice was hostile. "Does she? And what does she say? About me?"

"Oh," I said; I was very upset. "Oh. You know. The one night she came on about you. She said I had to watch you. She said you were a bitch."

I have never seen Jenny's face so vicious. "Well, up yours," she said, very quietly. "You can whistle for it, in future."

She stood up, and I said, "Look! I didn't say it! It's not me! It's her!"

She stopped by the door; I felt she was walking out of my life for good, though I didn't see why; I was crying; I supposed she was the only friend I'd got.

She said, "Thomas, darling, you want your bloody bumps feeling. You are going off your rocker, in case you haven't noticed. And I'm not coming with you. Bye bye."

It was hours before I slept; another night worming up and down inside of the egg; and then Christmas morning.

Father gave me a bicycle; Aunt Joyce cooked a turkey; Mrs. Jeffry left me alone for the day. I watched Jenny; I tried to pull a cracker with her; she avoided me, following the brothers off into the kitchen, leaving me to think about what they were doing in there. It was one of the worst days of my life.

In the afternoon, I sat beside the tree; the same tree, perhaps, that I had raided for chocolate, six years before. My auntie found me; she levelled one of her wan smiles in my direction, and sat beside me on the settee.

"Well," she said. "You do look miserable, today. Don't you like your bike?"

"Oh, I don't know," I said. "I mean, yes. It's great. It's – other things . . ."

"Yes," she said, and I remembered how beautiful she was. "Is it Jenny?" I didn't see how I could say anything at all, so I didn't; Joyce said, after a time, "She's too pretty for her own good, that one."

I didn't really know what she meant; indeed, I don't believe it, even now. Jenny isn't too pretty for her own good; she's too pretty for everyone else's, but not for her own. I carried on saying nothing.

"Don't let her bother you, Tom," she said. "They're just not worth it, in the end. Not that kind."

I couldn't understand why she was talking like this, to me, about her own daughter. I said, "Oh. That's all right."

"Good," she said, and smiled. When she smiled, she looked sadder than ever. She kissed me, then, very gently, on the lips. "I know how lonely you are," she said. "You've got nobody, you poor old thing. There's always me, Tom. If you need to have a talk to somebody. You can always find me."

I said, "Oh. Yes. Thank you." Then she went – to make a

turkey salad, I suppose. She had succeeded only in embarrassing me; I felt slightly angry, slightly hot; I didn't know a true friend when I saw one.

I told Jenny about that kiss, last week. My wife was away – visiting Aunt Joyce, in fact; there is an age difference, but they have become good friends. Jenny had just despatched me, expertly, in bed; being made love to by her is sometimes like being jointed by a skilled butcher. "Your mother kissed me, once," I said. "She was warning me off you."

"Yes," she said. "Well. She was right, wasn't she? You'd be better off without me, that's for sure."

Yes: they were both right about that. Jenny got out of bed in the silence; she wandered about, naked; I liked her better with clothes on – with a few clothes on, at any rate. She knew that – she knows everything about me, in that way. She began to dress; Jenny putting her clothes on is more erotic than any other woman taking them off. She leant against the bedroom wall, in her pants; she said, "I bet she didn't kiss you like I do."

I was angry at her presumption: angry at its accuracy. I said, "It wasn't that sort of kiss. She was trying to be motherly. It was that bloody Christmas, the one you wouldn't speak to me. She was trying to cheer me up."

"Don't you believe it," said Jenny, doing her bra. "You were quite a tasty little piece, at twelve. I fancied you like mad. Emerging puberty and all that."

I suppose that it is possible that I have not made it clear quite how much I hate my cousin Jenny. I detest her with the loathing of a prisoner for his gaoler; or with the revulsion of the addict for his drug. I cannot, on reflection, discover one decent characteristic in the whole of her agile, versatile body. I think I hated her always, even when I was twelve; but of course, when I was twelve, I didn't know it.

She queened it, all Christmas; she strutted around, filling the air between us with her completeness, fugging it, as with cigarette-smoke, pouting her indifference. She was certain that Mrs. Jeffry was just my own, tortured mind; the opinion that Jenny was a bitch was simply my own opinion, subliminally held. I was equally certain that this was not the case; it hadn't occurred to me, before then, that Jenny was a bitch; though, of course, she was. Oddly enough, it was at that point that it began to dawn on me; the prediction, as it were, fulfilled itself.

I was, therefore, on my own more than usual; and I didn't know Uncle Roger's house well enough to hide my solitude. I tried; I wandered about, and found a cellar; it had a washboiler in the corner, with a cast-iron oven under it. The top of the boiler was a big, cast bowl. Once, people had washed their clothes in it – people, servants, contemporaries of Mrs. Jeffry. It occurred to me that, at one time, when she was five or six years old, she had led a very alien life – a history-book life, with servants, perhaps, and gas lights, soldiers smart as toys. A life that, somehow, involved giant eggs.

Well, it doesn't sound very plausible; I accept that. I asked Joyce about it, on Boxing Day; I found her in the kitchen, her hands washing up, her face as blank as the moon. "How could there be," I asked, sitting at the table, with a cup of tea, "a sort of giant egg you could get into?"

She said, oddly, "How big?"

"Oh. It must be twenty feet high."

"Oh," she said. "I see. Have you – er – seen this thing, then, Tom? This egg?"

She stopped washing up and came to sit opposite me. We were alone; the brothers were competing, somewhere, for Jenny's interest; I don't know where my father was. I saw less and less of him.

I said, "I first saw it in a dream. I dream about it a lot. Jenny said it was Freudian, but it isn't."

Joyce smiled, studied her tea, watching the light in its surface. "Oh," she said. "Oh. A dream. Well," and she paused; I thought that she was really thinking about it. "No," she said. "I just haven't the faintest idea what that could be. I'm sorry."

We went home: back to Birmingham. Father started doing

his work; the brothers went off playing games; they loved sport. It was a biting cold evening right in the new year when my father visited me in my bedroom. It was surprising in itself; I really don't think he'd ever been in there before; he looked around, like a guest, wondering where to sit. As always, he spoke in a friendly, formal manner – like a bank manager dealing with only a slight overdraft.

"Don't you have, Tom, any friends you might like to bring home some time? For the holidays? I wouldn't mind, Tom. Boy or girl. You do seem so much on your own."

I said, politely. "Oh. Yes. Thank you. I'll have a think."

"Yes," he said. "Good." I noticed that he had a small moustache; I couldn't remember having seen it before, but he couldn't have just grown it. That wasn't the sort of thing he did. "Yes," he said. "You do seem to mooch about, you know." Well; it was true; I did. There was silence; then, surprising myself, I said: "What did happen, about the will? Mrs. Jeffry?"

He looked hunted; there was something going on, all right, though I hadn't mentioned the matter since the previous August. "Oh, Tom . . ." he said. "You shouldn't worry yourself about things like that."

I said, "No," but I wouldn't say "sorry" as well. I wasn't getting a fair deal; that was obvious. He said, quickly, "Anyway; I've got an idea for you. Little surprise."

I said, "Yes?"

"It's this bedroom of yours. I mean, you could hardly call it a bed-sitter, could you? No wonder you never bring any friends in. Lad of your age. So, I say, what about you moving out of here and taking up the big landing bedroom?"

I was worrying about his moustache, wondering where I might find an old photograph for comparison. He was watching me, oddly; I think I asked him about a photo; I can't remember. He said, "Well? Would you like that?" meaning the room change, and I was crying, frightened and angry, because he was trying to get me to move into dead Mrs. Jeffry's room, the one with the pouffe and the huge television-set; he seemed to be on her side. "I'm not going in there," I said, resentfully. "You can't make me do that."

I cried for some hours after he'd gone. I realise now that he was simply baffled; he'd only been trying to be kind; it was the first conversation we'd had for months, or perhaps years. He simply gave up, then; gave up trying to sort me out, and I wandered into Mrs. Jeffry's empty bedroom, her other empty bedroom, as it were, and had a look round. I expected her to get on at me, in there, in her territory; but she didn't. I suppose she didn't need to. It was patently clear then, as now, that for some reason Mrs. Jeffry wanted to break up the family; in some way, she wanted to appropriate me to herself. I don't know why. All she liked doing with me was hitting me. Anyway, whatever her motives, it was obvious what she was trying to do. And it was working.

7

She screamed at me. "No! No, Thomas, no! Keep it down! Down!"

Her hand was on the back of my head, holding my hair in a small loop. She was ramming my head in and out of the water, as if bouncing a tennis ball. "You're frightened of your own shadow!" she screamed, meaninglessly. I was drowning, in jerks; my forehead kept hitting the water, painfully, the sea rearing up and smacking me in the face. "You'll never do it," she said, "if you're going to be scared all the time."

I was scared but, more to the point, I was sick; my mouth stank of salt, my lungs seemed fully of dirty gas. "I don't want to . . ." I panted, when I could, but, as usual, she took no notice. I was eight years old; it was 1958; Mrs. Jeffry was teaching me to swim.

I staggered upright and looked back at the shore. She had quite suddenly given up, for a moment; I suppose she was tired. The beach was more or less deserted; it was April; the trippers weren't yet about, the little town was without purpose. It was a long, very gentle beach, popular in summer, because of its kindly shelf, and its particularly fine sand. People loafed about there, from July to September; youths hung over the pier railings; prim families stretched out below and tried to ignore them. But in April there were just a couple of dog-walkers, a man in a mac on the pier, paying us no attention, and Mrs. Jeffry was trying to make me open my eyes under water.

"You should know this," she said, panting slightly, up to

her knees in water. She must have been wearing a bathing-suit; I can't remember. It isn't an attractive thought.

"Your mother should have done this with you, years ago." She started it up, again; I went along with it, as best I could. I have already said that I don't like the water but, on the other hand, Mrs. Jeffry would have made anything else just as unpleasant. If we'd been sitting safely on sand, eating ice-creams, looking serene in the pale spring sunshine, she would have been muttering at me about this or that, leaning in to me, hissing.

I tried to open my eyes; I had supposed that they would sting, in the brine, but they didn't; they just felt stretched, as if someone were pulling the edges of them out towards my ears. I couldn't see anything; it was just like keeping them closed, but more uncomfortable, pointlessly demanding, like everything that woman did. I said they stung, even though they didn't; I had an instinct about her, even then; she seemed satisfied at that, and allowed me out. I got changed, behind a towel, with great self-consciousness; I hated her looking at me, coming into the bathroom without knocking, a little bit of mockery on her face. "A child should learn to swim," she said, drying herself, sitting on a deckchair, "before it's three."

I said, quite innocently, "Did you teach your children when they were three?" I was probably trying to do no more than make conversation; there were only the two of us; we had to pass the time somehow. But she was furious. "You know perfectly well that I've got no children," she said, and started reading a crime novel. I wandered off and spent some pocket-money at a kiosk; I was allowed to do that, so long as I didn't go out of sight. I bought a hot-dog, from a man whose hair was so greasy, he could have fried the sausages in it; the thought made me laugh. "I'm learning to swim," I told him. He said it was a mug's game; I didn't know what a mug's game was; life was full of phrases I didn't understand.

A girl wandered past the kiosk; the hot-dog-man said, "Will you look at that, then?" I looked; she was an alien, someone from another planet, a small tower, stiff, in a bikini. She made Jenny look ordinary; I suppose she was about sixteen –

twice my age. The man shouted, "Can I put some ketchup on it for you?" and she laughed, a huge, sliding laugh, sideways on her face, her mouth working laterally towards him, while she looked away. I was riveted, by the mystery, by understanding that I didn't understand at all. At eight years old, I watched her buttocks, protruding from the briefs; they made me think of my hot-dog, sticking slightly out of the roll, brown, warm. "My God," said the hot-dog-man. "Good God, nipper!" We seemed to be sharing something, so I smiled. "You want to try swimming in that!" he added, and shook a tray of frying onions, lifting them from the base they were sticking to. "Never mind," he said. "You'll see. One day." He laughed to himself; he didn't look at me, just as the girl had laughed without looking at him: why were people so secretive? "Yes," I said. An old dog was rabbiting about, above the shore; I followed him about for a bit, then I went home, back to the holiday house, leaving her on the beach by herself.

The old woman said, over supper, "Well. Not much of a swimmer." We seemed to be alone in her big house; I can't remember why; perhaps I'd been ill; they used to ship me down there to get over illnesses, occasionally; I suppose she was on hand to look after me.

I said, "'There was a very pretty girl, by the hot-dogs." It was an odd thing for an eight-year-old to say; I can quite see that. I could see it at the time. I was always testing her, trying her for reactions.

"Well," she said. "You don't want to worry about that." She ate her omelette, solemnly; it had cheese in it, melted in obscene strands that curled unctuously around her lips. I was eating a sandwich. "Time enough for that," she said. "I shall want a word or two. When you get interested in things like pretty girls."

I said, "Yes." I added, after a time, "I would best like to marry my mother." I was talking nonsense, trying to make amends for my erotic distraction.

She said, "Well, now. That would have been a fine time,

wouldn't it? A fine ceremony. Your pretty mother. Mind you, she was a bit tall for you, wasn't she? A bit of a bean-pole. A bit large. I don't suppose you remember."

It wasn't a question, so I didn't answer it. The fact was that she was right: after two years, I hardly did remember her; not in terms of physical details, anyway. Mrs. Jeffry added, "You'll be thinking about your cousin Jenny, one day, if I'm a judge."

Well; she wasn't, as far as I could tell, any kind of a judge at all, so I ignored her, as far as possible. I couldn't imagine how she could ever have any influence over me, when I was older. Eight-year-olds know they have to put up with that sort of thing; they imagine that the future will be different. I didn't know then that it would take me over a quarter of a century to shake her off, that she would still be moulding my life after she was dead.

Five years later, I sat on the great, stuffed pouffe in her room in the Birmingham house, wondering why she had told me she'd no children and, for some reason, worrying about my father's moustache, which seemed somehow connected. Perhaps there was a photograph in there; the old woman had plenty; she arranged us around herself, the cast of her own weekly drama. But I couldn't find one, so I went downstairs, and said I was sorry for fussing, and I would move into the vacant bedroom, and I asked him if he'd grown his moustache recently.

Father said, "Oh, Tom. I wish you wouldn't . . ." but I left him, because I couldn't understand, and lay on my bed, listening to my transistor radio – another Christmas present, from Uncle Roger. Mrs. Jeffry was on; she had cut out the records and was speaking to me, quite gently, telling me to watch them all. "You go into my room," she said. "You do as he says. You can keep an eye on everything, from there. That's what I used to do."

Well; it seemed a good idea. After all, there was no escaping her, wherever I went; that made no difference. And perhaps, in there, I might manage to sort something out, to comprehend what she wanted, to get rid of her. I fell asleep, and dreamed of the seaside, the big house; and, of course, the egg, its shell mazed and cracked, a texture of delicate rupture, like an old woman's face.

I went off to the Sales, in Birmingham, the day before the end of the Christmas holiday. I was supposed to get some shirts and socks; we didn't have the old woman to shop for us any more, and I was off to prove my manhood, venturing alone into the Bullring. It was disconcerting, in those days, to see rows of shops without cars; I didn't much like ramming myself into the little boutiques, stuffed with people looking sallow after Christmas, although the shop-girls seemed fabulous, the hair piled up, soft and stiff at the same time. I found the clothes easily enough; I found the bus home, out to our suburb with its substantial, Edwardian houses, proudly similar, discreetly different. It hadn't been a difficult expedition, though Father had made enough fuss; I was, after all, twelve years old.

I had three carrier bags; after a long walk past hedges, walls, fences, glancing at the gardens, tidied by the winter, well shaped by the sharp, January sun, I stopped and wondered which house was ours. By walking the whole length of the avenue, twice, I had managed to narrow it down to one of three. They stood adjacent to each other, and had bay windows of a particular type, which I recognised. Beyond that, I was lost. Father was out, the brothers were out; it would be hours before anyone arrived, to give me a clue; and I was feeling the cold. I had lived in the house all my twelve years; I had entered it tens of thousands of times; now I could not remember what it looked like, what it was called, what its number was. I sat on a low garden wall, and, quietly, I began to cry.

I half expected the old woman to start on at me, again, but she didn't. I sat on the freezing parapet of a garden wall until my thighs ached with it; the winter sun fastened the road, the pavement; frost coated the shadows, living exactly up to their edges. After about three-quarters of an hour, I stood up and walked inside, kicking my solid feet on the doormat, looking back at the coloured glass of the front-door window, sharp as ice. I made some tea, and lit the fire – we had no central heating, then; I went upstairs, and sat in my bedroom, trying to think about moving my books out into Mrs. Jeffry's old room, trying not to wonder whether I was going mad, and why.

I suppose I fell asleep. It was a good two hours later that I woke. I had been dreaming of drowning; of Mrs. Jeffry teaching me to swim, when I was eight. My mouth was warm, and wet; no air moved when I breathed in; my chest would not shift. I struggled to rise from the dream, reaching up in the dark for the surface, but my mouth remained trapped, locked into a depth; and, even when I awoke, my mouth was still not part of me. Its function was someone else's; and I began to cry again, but with relief, this time; for the someone else was Jenny, there in the flesh, not a dream at all; and kissing me with the ardour and caprice of the sea.

8

Doctor Lister said, "Yes. Well. We'll see what a little sea air will do!"

There was a cactus on his desk, between us; a tight, shapely, shiny bulb – like Doctor Lister himself. His smile grew like a fence; he stood up; he took me to the door, where Jenny and O'Cleary were waiting.

"Well," he had said, an hour before, rising, beaming. "Thomas. Thomas Fellows. Well now. Yes. Well. What's all this about then?" His fingernail was expert on the lines of notes; typewritten notes, surprisingly many of them, about my state of mind. Doctor Lister was a psychiatrist.

"Well, now," he said. "It seems you've been a little – upset. Yes. Well. Why don't you tell me about that?"

I had no option. I'd been shipped down there, to the holiday house, for rest, and for Doctor Lister, who knew his stuff. School had gone by the board, for me and for Jenny, too; she was to keep me company. Auntie Joyce was to look after us, paring out salads and tinned soup; and O'Cleary, now living in the lodge, didn't seem to mind ferrying us about.

Anyway, as I say, I had no option: so I told the doctor about coming home and not being able to recognise my own house for three-quarters of an hour; and, on being urged to go on, I told him that on some days my father seemed to have a moustache, and on other days, he didn't. Doctor Lister said it was interesting; then he asked me about my mother dying, and I told him about having known, somehow, in advance, and he said that was called a premonition, and quite common, and I needn't think that it meant I was psychic or anything similar. I said, truthfully, that the thought had never crossed my mind.

Doctor Lister said that that was useful, and asked me to go on, so I told him about Mrs. Jeffry; about how she had taken us over; about how she had grown thinner and iller; about how her skin had tightened while her clothes had loosened, her skirt flapping increasingly between her legs like an old pair of trousers. I told him how her face had shrunk so that her nose seemed to grow and her eyes to flicker with a manic, red life. He said that was interesting, too; he said it was called a step-mother syndrome, and not particularly unusual. We both knew that I was having a nervous breakdown; but Doctor Lister seemed to find it less disturbing than I did. I suppose he was trying to reassure me, but in fact I began to find his indifference irritating. So I told him that, seconds after her death, Mrs. Jeffry had spoken to me, her voice breaking out of the thin air.

He didn't write anything down; I kept looking at his notepad, but he seemed to be trying to memorise it all. I told him the lot; about how she had gone on to tell me she'd left me all her money; about how my father wouldn't admit it; about how she spoke to me constantly, in space, over the radio. She even interrupted other people, now; my father could hardly get a word in; she didn't trust anybody and, increasingly, neither did I. Doctor Lister watched me, with his smile. When I'd finished, he sat still, for the best part of a minute. It seemed a long time; I could hear him breathing. His shirt was very white. Then he said, "Yes. Well. We'll see what a little sea air will do!"

We drove back to the big house in O'Cleary's filthy car, trundling through the sea air, O'Cleary and Jenny laughing their heads off in the front. I leant forward, and O'Cleary shouted over his shoulder that us fellows must stand up for ourselves against these little squits of girls. Jenny seemed to enjoy the insult, and laughed even more loudly, and smacked the man on his knee. "Look out!" he yelled, and swerved deliberately off the road onto the promenade, which was a car-park. "Off you go!" he said. "You two have a walk and I'll see you later. Come down to my place. My humble abode. Come for tea!"

We got out, and Jenny strode off onto the deserted beach, and I said, confidentially, in through the square car window, "Mr. O'Cleary. Have you moved any of Mrs. – of your mother's things? Photographs? I mean, there's one I want to look at. Only it's very important. Can I have a look at it, later? I mean, when we come round?"

He looked at me; his expression was often like this; a confusing mixture of affection and gloat. I liked him gloating; I didn't mind him thinking that he'd won me over. He had.

"Well, now," he said. "Which picture is that, then?"

So I told him about the egg, and the dreams, and how somehow the photograph might prove that I wasn't completely mad; and that's all I told him. "Yes," he said, kindly; for the first time in what seemed like years, or perhaps a lifetime, someone was listening to me. "Yes. Well. I don't recall such a picture, young Tom. But then, I haven't really paid them much attention, to tell the truth. We'll have a jolly good look this evening."

I caught Jenny up; we looked at the derelict pier, gaunt and skeletal above the winter-grey sand. She made a joke about toffee-apples, and squeezed my hand; and I began to remember how it felt to be relaxed.

It had been a morning appointment and we walked back across the field to the house. I didn't know what the legal position was; the old woman was dead, yet we still seemed to be renting the place from her: we went back there for lunch. Joyce had made a cottage pie, and we said how nice it was; she served it and seemed somehow proud; and she watched me all the time I ate, saying, "All right, Tom?" I replied, a number of times, to the effect that it was all right; and I watched her anxious smile. She seemed to grow smaller, receding, clearing up the kitchen like a puppet: she seemed so small she could perch on the kitchen table, like a bird. Indeed, the whole table seemed to diminish; the salt and pepper were thimbles; the mats were stamps; a piece of Dutch cheese shrank to a dice; something trivial, to throw in a game.

To put it another way, I felt that I was growing; that my shoulders would have to insert themselves amongst the light fittings, soon; I would have to put an arm up a chimney, like Alice. I knew it was part of my illness; Alice's problem was that that she didn't understand reality, didn't understand when she was dreaming and when she wasn't. Even when I was crawling around my egg, or plunging into the stench of the sea, I knew if it was a dream. I knew that it couldn't last, if it was. Which, of course, was precisely why Mrs. Jeffry's voice frightened me so much.

Anyway, I knew that I was hallucinating again, or whatever it was, so I got out of the kitchen, and went up to bed, and neither Jenny nor Mrs. Jeffry seemed to want to pay me the usual sort of visit.

I lay there, on the bed; the cocoa-tin was in position, though it was too cold outside for rain, the rowans separate and brittle through my window. I thought of how Jenny had behaved, that afternoon, on the beach. After squeezing my hand, she had swung herself onto a cross-piece of the pier, curling round it; she had raised herself above it, on her arms, like a gymnast; then she had bent her legs up, too, so that her skirt had fallen back, showing her thighs, which were both square and round; and showing her pants, a little pair of white briefs. She had held herself there, for some seconds, and laughed, and said, "Enjoying the view?" and then we had both laughed, sitting side by side, Jenny leaning on a pillar. I said, "I wish it could always be like this, Jen," and she smiled, her eyes turning inward and secret.

"Oh, well," she said. "Never mind, Tom."

It was all anybody ever seemed to say to me.

O'Cleary said it again, or something similar, later on that day, when we went for tea. I asked if we could have a look for the photograph, but he looked oddly at me; then he looked at Jenny, whose mouth was in cake; a sort of signal passed. It was the look my father had given me, when I had asked about the moustache. "Now, then, Tom," he said, the Irish milk in his voice, his unshaven face somehow lyrical, "we don't want to be bothering about that."

I think that I was sure at that point about the photograph. I knew that I had seen it, before I had started to become confused; somehow, it seemed like an anchor, now, in my mind: a guarantee that things would get better. I said, "Oh, look, I would be very grateful if we could just have a look. I mean, if you say you haven't moved anything . . ."

O'Cleary said, "Look, Tom. You don't want to bother with all this, now. At your age . . . a lot of people go through this, you know. It's nothing to be ashamed of."

Jenny said, "Yes. He's right. You listen to him. He knows more about this than we do. I don't know. He seems more concerned about you than your own father. Forget about the picture. Just lay off. Like the doctor said."

O'Cleary hadn't altered the little sitting-room. It was still full of gaps, where things had been taken upstairs; but it seemed festive and secure, that evening, with a little fire burning, where Jenny was trying to make toast, O'Cleary helping her. I thought about the last time I'd been there, shining my torch around, like a burglar, discovering the man himself in the kitchen. I said, "Look. I'm sorry. But I want to talk about something. About the will."

I'd thought he would dismiss that, too, but instead he got up off the mat, gave me a crumpet, sat beside me on the little, floral settee. "Yes," he said. "Go ahead. It needs clearing up, does that."

I said, carefully, "I believe she left me everything. I don't know why she would do that, and I can't tell you why I believe it, either, but I do." There was silence. It occurred to me that Jenny might blow the gaff, like she had nearly done before; but they both sat very still, Jenny quietly eating, licking her fingers. "I don't like to ask it," I said. "Because I like you very much. But are you involved with this? I mean, do you know what's going on?"

He sat still for a few more seconds; then he leant towards me, and spoke very softly. He said, "Yes. There are complications. Definitely. Your father has asked me not to talk to you about that. That's his job."

I looked at him. I looked down at Jenny, who clearly knew nothing about it, shoving in the cake, the firelight golden on her bare knees. I said, "Why can't you tell me?" It wasn't that I wanted the money, or the houses. I just wanted to know who was telling the truth.

"No," said O'Cleary, again. "I can't, young Tom. That's your father's job. I'll tell you this, though," he added, after a pause. "There's not a penny left to me, in that will. If that's what you're thinking. If that's what you're worried about. Not a penny. Not a thing. Not the smallest thing." He looked genuinely hurt, just for a moment: he was telling the truth; I guessed that, then, and I know it for a fact, now. So I said, "Oh. I'm sorry. No. It isn't that . . ." and then I went upstairs, to the bathroom.

The landing light was on; I didn't need a torch, this time. The bedroom door was open, and I could see the photographs, the novels, even the television magazines, all untouched since last August. I could see the oval frame, too, on the windowsill; I could faintly make out the white smudge of the child; I dropped it into my jacket-pocket, terrified, flushed the lavatory, and ran downstairs.

"You're sure, about the photograph?" I managed to ask, casually, later on, as we were taking the plates through into the tiny kitchen. He said, "Tom. It isn't there. By all means, go and look, if you want. I'll come with you. Or you can go by yourself. Whatever you like. But there's no egg, old lad. I'm sorry."

I couldn't understand it. I had the thing in my pocket. I wanted to show it to him, and to her, to prove that a corner of my mind had remained unoccupied by fantasies. How could he rely on my saying, "Yes, I believe you"? Why did he want to keep it from me, anyway? Of what possible benefit could that be to him? I felt my hand begin to grow again, on my arm; my fingers began to inflate, like tiny, bulbous balloons; they began to press on each other, to turn sticky where they touched: I was having one of my turns. I had decided that O'Cleary was to be trusted, in a faintly dangerous sort of a way; now that seemed to be nonsense, too; he was telling me gratuitous lies, like everyone else. "You go home," he said then. "Rest is what you need. That's what it's all about. Jenny'll help me with the dishes," and quite soon I was on my own, sauntering up the rowan avenue in the parched, January darkness, listening to them laughing at something in the kitchen.

It was only nine o'clock, and I went through the house, and out the back, past the crab-apple where, only a few months before, I had begun my reticent celebration of Mrs. Jeffry's death; past the dry, empty willow which stuck like an obsolete spider web over the lawn's edge. I walked up the little mound which was beside the lake, striding slowly, my hand on the picture frame in my pocket; my only bit of solid evidence – though evidence of what, I think I had by then forgotten. Looking back, I cannot see the logic by which the picture proved or disproved anything: but it meant a lot, then; and O'Cleary's lies gave it an even greater importance. Feeling somehow heroic, I sat on the little wooden bench which had its back to the bricked-up air-raid shelter, and, sighing with relief, I looked out across the lake.

I hadn't realised until then that it was frozen. It was easily visible; the moon was absolutely full, and the lake shone, round and white, like the moon's facsimile, a tiny, lunar territory on which man had never walked; a terrain of perfect, ashen ice. I looked from the moon to the lake, and back again, seeing them joined by the thin line of the night; I felt the slow walking, the expert dream of the spaceman – even though, of course, there had at that time been no real spacemen at all.

I set off, walking across the ice, towards the tiny island in the centre. I had it in mind that O'Cleary would come looking for the picture, that I could hide it there; no-one ever walked on the ice, as far as I could remember. I had already stopped feeling the cold, except as a sort of exquisite thrill; I just heard my shoes scrape on the powder, watching them etch flecked patinas into the ice, wondering when it was all going to give way. I remembered that ice grew thinner as you got further out; I wished that Jenny had been there; this must have deserved a kiss.

I went on in my frozen movement, looking, I expect, like a statue, held by the white light from above and below; then I heard a voice, travelling slowly at me, catching me up: "Tom! Come back!" I didn't dare look around; I had to keep a perfect symmetrical balance, like a rope-walker; I reached the island, which is really just a tree, with some mud pressing its roots. I climbed onto it, and the extra push broke the scale of ice below one foot; but that didn't matter, since the picture was safe, and somehow walking back was much easier, Joyce calling, mournfully, "Tom! Whatever are you doing?", the moon and the lake locked into a single gaze.

I slept without dreams, without ghosts, only to wake up in the small hours to the sound of dripping, beside my head. The cocoa-tin was almost full. As is the manner of late January weather, the temperature had risen and, outside, the ice was melting fast.

9

I said to Joyce, "I suppose we won't be able to come down here, now." We were in the kitchen, the next day; outside, the snow had gone, the house was cascading, the edges blurred with brick-coloured rain. Through the kitchen window I could see the lake, the tree in the middle. I know now that it was no more than a pond; I could have waded it in minutes; but then it looked like a small, muddy ocean, the tree aloof. I didn't know what I was going to do.

Joyce was making coffee. "No," she said, after a time. "I don't suppose we will. Still. You won't miss it, will you, Tom? I won't. Awful old place."

She sat beside me, again. We often seemed to be side-by-side: fellow spectators, strangers to each other but joint participants in some sort of performance. I said, "No. You're right. I don't like this house, much. It's full of holes."

"How are you, this morning?" she asked, sipping her drink, blowing out a thin jet of visible steam into the cold morning air. "I mean," she added. "What a palaver. Wandering about on the ice in the middle of the night. What would Mrs. Jeffry have said?"

She smiled, and I giggled, and then she laughed, too: her laugh was as exuberant as Jenny's, though without the edge. We both chuckled on, for a few seconds; I realised then that we children weren't the only ones to have hated the old woman's dominance, to have been relieved when she died. "You shouldn't think ill of the dead," said Joyce, and I said, "No. But she was a hideous old bag . . ." and Joyce snorted with laughter so that coffee ejected from her mouth and bounced down her jersey and she banged her cup down violently into its saucer and said with a kind of mock seriousness, "Oh, yes. I'd have to admit that."

Her face was acquiring colour; in anyone else, it would have been a flush; in Joyce, it was the lifting of a kind of chill. I liked it; I said, "Yes. I mean, apart from being a hideous old bag, and a Jersey cow, with a brain like a porcupine, we mustn't think badly of her, now she's dead."

I don't know why she laughed so much; they were schoolboy jibes, the best I could do, only half-understood from the playground; but Joyce was helpless. She blew her nose on a Kleenex and said, "Stop it, Tom!" and I said, "Sorry. You're right. I won't say another word about the old bat," and she started laughing again, and I was laughing, too, our heads leaning into each other, our shoulders touching, when Jenny came in.

It occurred to me fleetingly that she might be jealous, just for the interest, just for the enjoyment of it; but instead, she said, "What's all this?" and I said, "We were just paying our last respects to the most obnoxious old lady it has ever been our misfortune to come across," and then we were all three laughing, stupidly, childishly, while Jenny made her own breakfast, slopping egg after egg into a frying pan, impersonating the old woman uncannily, in a way I didn't know she could: "Come on, now, Thomas, lad. Your lovely mother should have fried you some of these appalling, greasy old eggs in four inches of filthy chip-fat of a morning! This'll put hair on your acne!" O'Cleary came in the back door, apparently without knocking; he smiled at us; but it was our joke; it was really for Joyce and me. We all shut up, straight away; Jenny looked embarrassed; Joyce didn't. He said, "Oh, dear. Am I interrupting something?" His eyes twinkled; rain ran merrily on his nose; he was a liar.

Jenny said, "Oh. Hello, Tom," meaning O'Cleary, not me. She kissed him, on the cheek, like a daughter; I noticed that she was only wearing her nightie. He thinks he's a member of the family, I thought. Well, he's not. He can stick it. Like his mother.

"I'm thinking of running out to Wyston," he said. "Little pub out there, for lunch. Any chance of a bit of company?" Joyce said, "Oh, thank you. I'm far too busy here. But the kids . . ." Jenny said, "Great!" and shot off upstairs to dress; I said, "No, thanks. I don't think I'll bother, today."

Joyce looked worried; perhaps she wouldn't have let Jenny go with the man, without me; now it was too late to say anything, without seeming rude. She said, "Go on, Tom!" but at that time, I didn't understand her discomfort, and I certainly wasn't having anything at all to do with a man who told me he hadn't got what he had got when having it meant nothing to him but a great deal to me. "Sorry," I said. "Don't feel like it." I knew they couldn't argue; I was to avoid all stress.

O'Cleary said, "Oh, well. Fine"; Joyce said, "Are you sure, Tom?" and after a time they set off, leaving me sullen and vaguely jealous in the kitchen. I was angry with them both; Jenny, for preferring to spend time with somebody else; and O'Cleary, for nearly proving a good friend and turning out to be a false one.

I was in the billiard room, glumly trying solitary shots, the clicks of the balls like spots in the silence, when Joyce came in and plugged in the hoover. The noise made everything impossible so I leant on the wooden rim of the enormous table and watched her and watched the rain, viscous on the tall, sash windows.

When she switched the machine off, the silence was awful, a mad rushing in the brain; I felt dizzy, and hot. Joyce said, very distinctly, "You do not marry Jenny. Jenny is not for marrying. When you are older, you may make a mistress of her, if you wish. You may have no choice. But when you want to get married, there must be someone else."

It was like a recitation; a part of the day that didn't belong with the rest of it. After a time, in which neither of us moved, or looked at the other, I said, "Was – was that you? Did you say that, then? About Jenny?"

It had occurred to me that it might have been Mrs. Jeffry; she might have taken to impersonation, though it would have been the first time. But Joyce looked at me, and said very steadily, moving her lips, as if I were deaf: "I say what I think, Tom. I am very fond of you, though I don't see you much. There isn't much time to beat about the bush. So I say what I mean. It may mean little to you, now; one day, it may mean a lot."

It was the most extraordinary conversation I had ever had in my life, in that it didn't resemble a conversation at all; and, furthermore, I hadn't much idea what it was about. I looked at Joyce for some seconds more; she was pale, again, and, because I didn't like that, I found myself saying, "Dearly beloved. We are gathered here together at the Cleethorpes crematorium and abattoir to mourn the passing of a geriatric old battleaxe who turned misery into an art-form and lived until she was seventy-eight, which was about seventy-seven years too many . . ." And Joyce was laughing again and looking grateful and the sun was having a bit of a go through the clouds.

I avoided him for about ten days; I gave up trying to work it out, and skulked about in the garden, when it was dry, or wandered about on the sands. I didn't see much of Jenny; she and the Irishman were great friends, though they pretended they wanted my company; they were off on day-trips, all the time. He didn't seem to have a job, like Father. Joyce just hoovered and smiled, but I was worried about her, too. I stored her message, verbatim, ready for a future time, when I might be able to decode it.

Although I was very lonely, I began to feel better. I said this to Doctor Lister, on my second visit; I said that I was beginning to see things differently. I told him that only days before I had walked across an iced lake in the dark, thinking it was important; it seemed ridiculous, now. I told him that it was a long time since Mrs. Jeffry had spoken to me; the pressure of the air above my head seemed to be lifting; I looked upwards more often and more easily; I told him that I could sniff spring in the February air. I was, I think, an articulate boy. As usual, Doctor Lister wrote nothing down; I couldn't think why he wasted money on notebooks if he never used them. Instead, he smiled, and stood up, and said that it was interesting.

I walked back, that time; you could do the whole distance on the beach, though it was a long way round; I grinned up at the old pier and, standing still – it was a particularly windy day – I could watch the whole structure waving about. It had apparently become more dangerous since the summer: various supports were giving way, submarinely, invisibly; the green, dank water was getting at it. I didn't mind; I felt glad that I'd walked it when I did; I even felt grateful to Jenny, for making me do it.

The problem with Jenny was that, whatever anybody might say about her, she mattered to me; and nothing else did. That is to say that the many other things that did matter – doing well at school, getting a decent meal, avoiding rugby, not upsetting Father – mattered on an entirely different scale. For example, I was beginning to find a friend in my Auntie Joyce. She seemed, unaccountably, to like me; she had said the other day that, breakdown or no breakdown, I was saner than the rest of them. But the extent to which that was in any sense important was an extent which faded to nothing before the extent to which Jenny's mouth was important even began. It was an entire sexual obsession, with Jenny. It still is.

Anyway, I stared up at the pier, and after a time I realised that you could see the hole, now, about two-thirds of the way along its length; the hole through which a girl had fallen to drown; the hole through which, it struck me, I had nearly done the same. I felt frightened, just for a minute – more so than I'd been on the night itself; I think that just for a second or two it crossed my mind that this had been more sinister than a schoolgirl dare. In the daylight, when there had been no hole, a girl had died; and Jenny had sent me out there, in the pitch dark, with the hole ready and waiting. When I'd come back, she had applied herself to me, smeared desire onto my face so that it would never disappear. It never has.

My new-found lightness of heart began to ebb pretty quickly. I got home, and found myself alone; Joyce and Jenny were shopping. Using a system of swimming trunks and a long pole, I made my way slowly across to the tree in the lake, the pole sounding the depths in front of me; at its worst, the water only reached my thighs, and soon I was back in the kitchen, soaking, shivering, with the photograph, which I hadn't actually looked at since I'd stolen it, days before.

Well; it wasn't, of course, an egg. The frame was oval, like many Victorian picture-frames; and there was a little girl at its centre: Mrs. Jeffry, certainly; the peeved face was unmistakable. She was, I should think, seven or eight years old; she was dressed in white, sitting on a swing, in a garden; the kind of swing that hangs from a tree. I could even recognise the tree; she must have come to the big house at a very early age. But she was not sitting in a giant egg; nor did she look in any way at all as though she could have been mistaken for someone sitting in a giant egg, not even by a frightened little boy, not even at night; not even by torchlight. Or, at least, not by a frightened little boy who was in his right mind.

10

The next week was the happiest I have ever had. O'Cleary, Jenny and I waltzed up and down the empty, winter coastline, watching the dim rain eroding the landscapes, charging into pubs with children's rooms; we did a sort of conga around the estuary. The man wasn't a liar, after all; there had, indeed, been no photograph; Jenny was right to trust him, and I was happy to find her so, and we drank small amounts of beer, and caroused in a medieval sort of way, fetching up in cove after cove in the old Morris.

The old woman continued to leave me alone; Jenny's clothes became increasingly outrageous; she took to wearing make-up, and danced a lot, outside, behaving like a hippie, years before anyone had thought of them. The entire week was a song; that is how I still remember it; my body singing with relief. It was a relief to know that O'Cleary had told me the truth, even if that meant that I'd been deluded before. Indeed, after all the heart-searching, it was even a kind of relief to accept the delusion. I'd been imagining things; I'd had a breakdown; it was a kind of release, in itself; a release from logic and responsibility. And, of course, I had a friend: the first one in my life.

"Yes, indeed!" he shouted at me, one evening, shouting from the kitchen. He made washing-up look like juggling; life with him was a circus. "The Watney's is what I would call personally an insult to the intelligence. That one'd like it of course. What else can you expect, from a woman?"

Jenny, sitting beside me, shouted, "Well, I say it was nice!" and then she began to kiss me, her mouth worming away, her hand beginning to suck at my trouser-leg. She stopped kissing, withdrawing her mouth like a cork, to shout, "Tom enjoys it! Don't you, Tom?" and I was helpless, only partly with laughter, because she had withdrawn her mouth only, not her hand. "Don't you like it, Tom?" she shouted again, and I had to gasp, "Yes. Yes, yes, I do!" and O'Cleary laughed in the kitchen and shouted back, "I hope that's the beer he's talking about in there!" and I was suffocating because I wanted to laugh into Jenny's warm throat. She seemed never to need to breathe. Our internal organs seemed simply to link into a sort of erotic symbiosis.

O'Cleary came in, drying his hands, and burst out laughing at the sight of us. "Good God!" he yelled, striking his forehead. "I've just remembered I've got to service the car and read *War and Peace* this evening! See you later," and he disappeared again. Jenny had her hand on my neck; she rammed my eyes down to her breasts, my nose was smelling the soapsuds of her bra; this was all completely new – to me, at any rate. I said, "What – ?" and she said, "Shut it!" and sat up suddenly, as if she'd changed her mind.

I said, "Sorry . . ." but she said, again, "Shut up! Bra . . ." and then I saw that her hands were behind her, inside her sweater: another circus act: escapology. I was sitting there, watching her fumble, watching the distracted concentration on her face, watching the end of her skirt as her knees joined and parted, when my father walked in.

For a moment, it seemed as though the circus would carry on: my father austere, like a ring-master, rigid in the centre of the room; Jenny and I fumbling like forlorn clowns, grabbing at falling trousers; the silence blasting on like a brass section. Then O'Cleary came in, and Father said, "What . . .?" and Jenny said, "Oh, God," and shame and embarrassment began to stoke themselves up into anger somewhere at the back of my neck.

O'Cleary said, "Look. It's just the lad . . .", but nobody could finish a sentence. I just looked at the wall opposite, while at the edge of my eye Jenny continued to adjust herself. Eventually, my father said, to O'Cleary, very quietly, "Just shut up. Be quiet. Don't you touch him, this lad. Don't let me see you have anything to do with him."

I don't know at what point this was said. A lot of other things were also said, by everyone but me. I didn't have the vocabulary for a scene like this one; I hardly seemed a part of it at all; just someone to clear up after the lions.

Anyway, my father told O'Cleary to leave me alone; Jenny said she didn't see what all the fuss was about, we weren't babies, her mum wouldn't mind, anyway; O'Cleary did as he was told. He kept quiet. After a while, I was up at the big house, alone in the kitchen with my father; Jenny was elsewhere, with Joyce. I was becoming increasingly upset; my shame was boiling up now with another bitter ingredient: sexual frustration. I couldn't forget the smell of Jenny's breasts.

My father said, "I don't suppose you know. Do you? About babies."

Of course I didn't. A few weeks ago, a popular magazine had published an interview with some film actress who had said that in America girls of twelve went out with boys; they had "dates". It had been such an extraordinary notion that it had grown into a brief, national obsession: people talked about it, everywhere. It wasn't so much the morality of the thing; it was rather that, in those days, it seemed a physical impossibility; a phenomenon. That was the world, then; that was the context in which my father found me, on the sofa with Jenny; a world five years away from the swinging sixties.

So, I didn't know about babies, or anything much of that sort, except that the whole issue was funny, or embarrassing, or exciting, depending on who was talking about it. My father told me about fine feelings; then, for some reason, he switched to bulls and cows – which, as far as I knew, had no fine feelings at all. I was desperately upset and confused; I shunted all my reactions to one side and dropped coldness into their place. I was monosyllabic: and, after twenty minutes or so of cows, bulls and babies, I was none the wiser, either. He concluded with: "So. I hope you'll understand that it's best for you not to see Jenny, for some time at least. Time enough for that, when you're older." "That" involved marriage, amongst other things; they didn't know that I knew that Jenny wouldn't marry me in a thousand years. Nor I her, I realised, as I sat in the darkening kitchen looking at Father's white face. That was not the nature of our relationship.

What I could see was that I was being isolated even further. I had been taken out of school; O'Cleary had been warned off; now it was Jenny's turn. I was in no doubt at all that the will was bound up in all this: Father was systematically depriving me of all friends, all witnesses, all sources of advice.

I said, "These people are my friends." I didn't feel repentant or disgusting – although I was, of course, embarrassed. I said, "I haven't got many friends. You said so yourself."

He sighed, and sat back: it was an eerie conversation; the house wasn't suited to it; the kitchen was usually untidy, cheerful and muddy; I was used to it in daylight. "I know, Tom," he said. "But you have to understand. Things . . . things aren't always what they seem." He seemed more embarrassed than I was.

I said, darkly, "Yes. I know. People don't always tell the truth."

He said, "No. Yes. That's right. I'm sorry . . ."

I said, "O'Cleary said you'd told him to keep quiet about the will. What is it? What's going on?" The fact that he was almost a stranger seemed to make it easier to press a point.

He said, very slowly, "Tom. Listen. The will." He cleared his throat, as if about to make a public statement. "You are not mentioned in the will," he said, a pause after each word. "I know you think you are. But you aren't. It absolutely does not concern you." He sat still for a very long time, not looking at me. Then he shifted, stretched, and stood up. "Tomorrow, you can go back to school," he said. "The doctor says you're better."

I sat there, in the dark, looking at the unexpected shadows, the moon slicing about the place; and I waited for the old woman. This was when she started, usually: at times of emotional stress. Doctor Lister had pointed that out. He thought she was a guilt complex, or what he called a "mechanism" for dealing with crises. She wasn't any such thing, of course. She helped me with absolutely nothing at all. On the contrary; she was a crisis herself.

Anyway, she said nothing. It had been a long time, now; perhaps she really had finished with me; perhaps she would leave the air empty, now, so I could breathe it, and taste it, and look through it like everyone else. Sitting there, alone in the kitchen, I watched the solid light scraping the walls; I heard my father tidying up, then going upstairs; I tasted the empty air, cold and white, like milk.

My sleep was liquid, too: pure and clear, like spring-water. I should have been troubled, I suppose; Doctor Lister would surely have thought so; but my head was light with the absence of Mrs. Jeffry and the renewed belief in O'Cleary, her son. I knew that the ban couldn't last. It may be fathers who originate such things, but it is mothers who keep them going, who translate attitudes into routines, and I didn't have one. After a few weeks, life would creep back to normal: there simply weren't enough people around me to prevent it.

So I slept an empty sleep, and in the morning I moved through great columns of solid air, leaving the house behind, screwing my eyes against the perfect, February whiteness of the sand, the opaque sea. I saw Joyce's car disappear, early in the morning; I didn't attempt to say goodbye; it didn't seem proper. I wandered up the bank, to the pier entrance, where a man in overalls stood, surveying, his hands up to his eyes, like a pirate captain. "It's a bright one!" he said to me, meaning the weather, steadying himself on the wooden barrier. He wrote something onto a clipboard; then he cocked one leg over the fence, as if climbing into a field. I said, "Be careful. There's a big hole, about a third of the way down. It goes almost the whole width."

"Yes," he said. "So I believe. Thank you very much. For the warning." He smiled. People often laughed at the way I spoke. I think it was rather formal.

"They're going to pull it down, are they?" I said. It was obvious. The sea was sucking away at the wood, digesting it bit by bit – while, on top, the old pier had less and less actual function. There was a large playpark, now, across the town; a fairground open all season, squashed full with mechanical horrors and prize-machines. There was only one way for the pier to go: eventually, it would lurch, stagger, flop like a kneeling skeleton, and dispatch itself in bits into the silky water. I didn't mind; I wasn't sentimental. I wanted to watch it go, though; as Doctor Lister would have said, that would have been interesting.

The man had disappeared, onto the pier, without answering, so I stood, and watched him – that was easy, of course, in the daylight. He made some notes – he kept his pencil behind his ear; then he hinged himself back out, onto the solid lumps of dry mud where the grass never got started. I said again, "Are they pulling it down?" and he said, "Oh, yes. Yes," and walked off towards the car-park, whistling. I wondered, casually, whether I would see the pier again. Today, it was back to Birmingham; tomorrow, back to school; for all I knew, we would never holiday in the big house again.

I watched the sea for a few moments – watched it with my usual distaste. It has never seemed to me symbolic of anything, much – certainly not of fruitfulness and life, though, five years later, I proposed to someone on that same beach, and she accepted me. The sea was a shapely backdrop on that occasion – folded, like a grey curtain; perhaps it made me feel romantic. In any case, at the age of eighteen, I stood there, near where the pier still lurched and hovered, and became engaged to a girl called Sally.

11

It wasn't unusual to find no-one in the ticket-office. There was only one man for the whole station, and he was usually strolling about, weeding his flower-beds, doing things with metal buckets. I never saw anyone else attempt to buy a ticket, anyway; people got off the train at Newport; they didn't seem to get on. In any case, I had my season-ticket; so I passed the tiny guichet and, since it was a bright summer day, I sat down on a platform bench.

It was a station, not a halt, with tiny, wooden buildings: verandas and banisters, all painted in red and yellow stripes. It was like a little fairground, like the entrance to a ghost-train ride; only its permanent emptiness jarred with the noisy colours. On that particular day, I couldn't even see the station-master, or whatever he was called; so I sat back against a wooden wall, looking up and down the single track which was scorched bright by absent movement.

There were some wires overhead, which normally gave off the odd grasshopper-song; today, even they were quiet; the sun pushed its light down uninterrupted, squeezing its way between the platforms, seeming to press them apart. I could have done with an ice-cream, or a drink of lemonade.

I was on my way to a weekend with O'Cleary: one of my illicit jaunts. I had become, in school terms – the terms of an obsessive, closed community – a criminal. I told enormous lies to everyone. I told Father that I was weekending at school for extra tuition or rugby; I forged notes requiring my presence at home, and handed them to Faceache, who barely glanced at them. Between the two of them I slipped, relying on Father's increasing evasiveness and school's fierce isolationism to keep them apart. I spent weekend after weekend with O'Cleary; sometimes, whole weeks, Whitsuns packed with the twinkle, the sips of beer, the packets of crisps. Often Jenny was there, too, and the three of us jammed into the lodge and O'Cleary increasingly turned a blind, twinkling eye.

I felt no shame whatsoever about any of it. I had learnt deception from the adults, and now I was using it against them. I was always a quick learner.

The train was late, but I didn't mind. I had all day, and it was always empty, an empty tube hurtling south, leaving the midland cities still packed behind it, and me sitting inside, facing oddly sideways across the route.

My mind was already occupying that sunlit carriage; I had been waiting for four weeks for this particular day to unfold itself; I had rehearsed the details of it. I was fifteen, at that point; Jenny, at seventeen, had left school, and she was going to be there, to sit on O'Cleary's knee, and tease him like a mischievous niece, and, if I had my way, gently to unburden me of my virginity.

I think that I drifted into a sleep. It is easy, in a railway station: easy to fantasise: it is so like a foreign country, where life peels itself away, where people jaunt around like dolls. Certainly, my eyes didn't close; but the arch of the sky folded over me, as I sat, holding the light over me, pressing meaning away, and I started to think about Jenny and the smell of her thighs and the thin, straight texture of her forehead.

She walked towards me and placed one finger – the index finger of her left hand – on the slim ledge of her hip. She was naked, and the hip closed against her side, a limpet shell, white as bone. The finger moved, laterally, pointing out the band of the waist, moving in towards the groin, pointing down. Her eyes didn't leave mine; she didn't need to look down; she knew what she was doing. The finger crept, back and forth, from the hip to the belly, absolutely erotic in its straightness: a perfect, climbing horizon. She said, "Watch. Watch. Watch," and I longed for the finger to dip, to sauce itself below the strict line; but she was too clever for that. What the finger didn't do was to be my struggle; I knew that: concessions were not to be made. "Watch!" she said, and, supplicant, I did as I was told, gazing across the narrow well of the vacant railway, at an advertisement for Brooke Bond tea, wishing she was not just a dream: hoping that, soon, she wouldn't be.

The train was an hour late, and I began to saunter around, mainly out of boredom, but partly in the hope of finding the man and asking what was going on. He was nowhere at all; the sun had shifted its angle; it was propping itself against the wooden roof; soon, it would begin to pour shadows over the day's promise. The afternoon was stretching itself.

I sat in the waiting-room, for a change, looking at a calendar, open to the wrong month, with a picture of a station – not Newport; a large, city place, full of expert travellers, trains lounging about punctually, prestigious, like lions.

I was thinking about her again when I began to realise that the train wasn't coming; no trains were coming; there was a small notice on the ticket-office telling me that the Ministry of Transport had closed the station and that, incidentally, I was trespassing. I hadn't seen it before. It was after five o'clock; officially, I was nowhere. Father thought I was at school; Faceache thought I was at home; I was stuck between them, with no money, either. I only had my season-ticket, which O'Cleary bought me every year; thanks to Doctor Beeching, that was useless: and, thinking of the finger, of her promise to sort me out this weekend – "Remember Toby," she'd said – I began to cry, again. I felt immensely sorry for myself: fifteen years old, with no real centre at all, except O'Cleary, who was perched two hundred miles away on the top of a railway-line.

I hadn't heard from Mrs. Jeffry for three years, but she came in, now; she walked into the shadow in the corner of the waiting-room, and stood still. I'd never seen her, before; not since her death, I mean; I peered carefully at her; there was no mistake. Death had pointed up the nose even further, had pushed the wrinkles of the skin into tight concertinas. Ghosts are supposed to have transparent skin but hers was rucked and solid, little mounds on the cheeks, pulled back from the eyes. She took a step or two towards me; I could hear her old skirt flapping; she wasn't silent. "Hello, Mrs. Jeffry," I said; I felt oddly comforted.

There was a table in the centre of the room, and she sat beside it, and I sat opposite her, my face two feet from hers. She looked always down, at the wooden surface; she clasped her hands, and watched them; then she began to speak.

She said, ridiculously, "Well, then. I expect you're pleased to see me? Oh, yes. I expect so." The night was dropping round us, like a top-hat: silk, flush, expensive. I wasn't frightened at all; it was an enormous relief to be face to face. I had thought of her, nightly, ever since I'd been twelve, and Jenny's hand had swum at my knee, and my father had come in; she had become a sort of prayer, something to be dealt with of an evening, a routine, like a cat to be put out. Now she sat so near to me that I could smell her; and, I have to say, that although she did not look transparent; although she was not silent, not moving like a tiny segment of a nocturnal graveyard, she did, nevertheless, smell slightly of death. There was a slight, pale sourness in the air, the sense of petfood in an old tin; and the silk blouse had been worn a long time; and the tweed of the skirt was well clogged up with age. She held the room quite still: I knew that, trespassing or not, nobody would disturb us.

"Off you go, now," she said. "Don't trust the lad. My son. He's not to be believed." It wasn't the enigmatic, obstructive speech of three years before; it had dry purpose instead of venom. "Find out the girl," she said. "Your cousin Jenny. She will lift you into all happiness."

It was a satanically lyrical phrase: "Lift you into all happiness." It seemed to me then that if anyone could do such a thing, it would have been Jenny. I said, "What about my father?"

Well; if a ghost can walk, and rustle its skirt, and smell, and move a wooden chair to sit down, then I suppose it can spit. If it can rattle chains, after all, then it can spit. That's what Mrs. Jeffry did, at any rate, with the sedate foulness of the middle-aged gypsy. "That," she said, having done it, "is what your father cares for you."

I said, "What are you doing here, now, after all this time?" I was genuinely surprised, because, although I was disappointed, and sexually frustrated, I wasn't exactly undergoing a crisis.

"Oh, well," she said, and smiled. "Time isn't exactly so important where I am," and it occurred to me then that I was talking to a dead person, that I was scenting a body which I had last seen in the form of a thin column of black smoke lifting above a chimney. I started to tremble.

"Go to the girl," she repeated, "your cousin Jenny," and, because I could think of nothing else, I did so, hitch-hiking to another station, waiting an hour and a quarter for a night train, changing all over the place, hitch-hiking again at the other end and finally walking three and a half miles to O'Cleary's lodge. I fetched up there at about nine-thirty on the next morning, a Saturday: about a day late.

It was an absolutely beautiful morning, though freezing cold; the walking warmed my body, but not my feet, and I was anxious to get inside, by the fire. Nevertheless, I did delay enough to have a glance at the sea, which was still and blue – blue with the cold of early summer, early morning. By midday the beach would be packed and roasting; already, half a dozen families were staking their claims, despite the lengthy, morning chill. The pier was still there; every year men wandered onto it, and tutted, and made notes; it was always about to be pulled down, but I suppose the council found better ways to spend its money. Perhaps they thought that it would collapse, eventually, of its own accord, thus saving them a job. There were barriers all round its base, by then, as well as its entrance; you couldn't sunbathe near it, or swim beneath it – in case it fell on top of you.

I waved down to one or two people I knew by sight – regular holiday-makers; one family in particular used the big house, though we didn't seem to any more. The brothers had left home, by the time I was fifteen; I lived with Father, and he sent me on summer camps with school, or adventure holidays, full of rock-climbing and canoes. Or he thought he did.

I let myself in to O'Cleary's – he had given me a key and there he was, on the landing, in his dressing-gown, full of it. "We thought we'd lost you!" he yelled, and, "Jenny, it's Tom!" and minutes later, she appeared, standing at the top of the stairs in a nightie, her legs bare, her feet apart, laughing at me. "Good God!" she said, "What a state!" and they both looked after me, laughing, energetic, so that by eleven o'clock we were all three on the beach: Jenny reading a magazine, O'Cleary sipping beer and watching the girls; and me, exhausted, falling asleep in the June light.

I slept soundly that night, too, with Jenny beside me. "She will lift you into all happiness," the old woman had said; and she had, that evening, carefully, lifting me with her arms and her hips, winding up a spring inside me which still ticks away now, uncoiling slowly, like a snake.

PART TWO

12

"He's not so bad!" said the girl called Sally. "I can't see what you're so desperate about." She was whispering; Father, about whom she was talking, was making coffee in the kitchen. He was making a great effort too; chatting away in his odd, stilted style, entertaining at the Birmingham house the first girl I had ever brought home. She was eighteen, the same as me; I had met her at university.

"Shut up!" I said; but she was right to be surprised. I hadn't told her much of the family history but I'd made it plain that this dinner was a duty, that Father was tedious, that I didn't trust him. Mrs. Jeffry hadn't bothered me for three years, since that night on the disused railway station; but I still found myself believing her about the will. I'd long ago given up caring, in any practical or material sense. The question all along had been that of who was telling the truth. O'Cleary's hint, together with Father's absolute denial, had cleared that up, as far as I was concerned. But I still had to live somewhere, between terms at Exeter, where I had found myself studying for a degree in Latin. So here I was, with this very small, dismissive girl, who had fascinated me in tutorials; who had amazed me by saying "Yes" when I'd invited her home for the weekend.

Father seemed to relax with her; he made jokes; he stopped looking bemused. I knew that, later, he would mention to me quietly that she was the "right stuff": that was how he talked. Meanwhile he was dealing out liqueurs, charming her all over the place, annoying me enormously – not with jealousy, but frustration that he was acquitting himself so much better than I'd led Sally to expect. It made me look silly.

I'd wanted, really, to take her down to O'Cleary, but Jenny was there, more and more, and that would have been awkward. Jenny seemed to think I was going to marry her, after all; I knew that I wasn't; but why either of us should think as we did, and just where Sally came into it, if she did, were matters I wasn't yet ready to draw to a head. So we went up to Father's.

"Super," he said; a word he never used; a ridiculous word. "Tom's such a dark horse, usually. About friends, and so on. Such a pleasure to see you." He gave us both Tia Maria; I knocked it back in one; I'd been used to drinking since I was about thirteen. Sally sipped. She was one of the smallest girls I'd ever seen, but you had to study her carefully to notice it. Her face was practical, her hair hung, well-cut, unfussy, about her cheekbones. They were the focus of her face; high, prominent cheekbones, above a straightforward mouth.

"Good stuff," she said, and smiled at him, just as she smiled, sometimes, at an idea in tutorials; a simple expression of pleasure, entirely without flirt or deceit. I hadn't seen much of her, but she seemed incapable of dissembling; I suppose that that was why I chose her.

We did the washing-up together in the gaunt kitchen; the Birmingham house was never like a home; more like an institution, with high windows; Sally said to me, "You should get him out of this awful place. He's nice. What's he do?"

I said, as lightly as I could, "He's an old fraud. That's what he is."

She looked at me very intently, a plate in her hand folded motionless inside a tea-towel. "Oh, no, he isn't," she said. "Don't be silly."

Her concern in bed that night was bewildering. I was used only to Jenny, who ordered the entire event, placing me into position as if I were a puppet, so that I seemed to move of my own accord, but didn't really. Sally put on pyjamas so that she looked even more like a child, and poured herself over me, like water against a rock. Afterwards she smiled simply and said, "Mmm. Good stuff," and went to sleep, while I lay and looked around my bedroom. After a time, I got up, and stared at the empty television – Mrs. Jeffry's old television; it had never been taken out. I studied my face in it, which I could see quite clearly. I wasn't bad-looking, at eighteen; average, with regular features; but it occurred to me that I looked very old: about forty, I thought. I looked very staid, for nineteen-sixty-eight; I didn't have long hair; I didn't wear beads; I looked like someone after a job in a bank. I thought of Jenny, who wore the tiniest of skirts, now; the exhibitionism of the mini-skirt craze might have been invented for her; she loved to bend over near groups of strangers and glare at them when they peeped. It was outrageous but, it occurred to me then, it was more normal than I was. And much more fun. I realised, sitting there in the middle of the night, looking at a reflected ghost, that I was rather a boring person. Behind me, the girl called Sally stretched an arm rigid across the bed. She had something to do with my discovery.

On Sunday, we drove back down to Exeter, down through Gloucester and Tewkesbury: there was no M5, then. I had already decided to marry Sally, at some point, although I'd known her less than a month. I had long ago decided against Jenny; being married to Jenny would have been like drinking a bottle of whisky at every meal.

Father hadn't mentioned her, again. For five years, she had been non-existent, or just a distant relative. Her parents, Roger and Joyce, had been to see us a couple of times, but Jenny was always busy elsewhere. Likewise, O'Cleary was a man we'd once met. We weren't the type of family that discussed crises, or brooded over them. We had them, and then we'd never had them; they mustn't interfere with mealtimes, polite conversation between Father, the brothers and me.

We had lived like that for five years, then: my father entirely ignorant of my continual, exuberant relationship with those whom he thought he'd banished. Similarly, he had no idea of how the brothers had come to dislike me. First, I had appropriated Jenny – their territory; then, by my excesses, I had debarred them from seeing her. They didn't know, either, that I spent weekend after weekend in increasing intimacy with her; that, when I was fifteen, she performed an expert initiation. I suppose that it was just as well.

I wanted to marry this Sally, partly because I was sick of the lot of them. I knew then that I would never be free of desire for my cousin; I could see that that would be a problem. I thought, too, that O'Cleary would always be my best friend; but, for the rest of them, I was tired of families; I still am. They seem weary and difficult, little bands of banal desperadoes huddled together, conjuring rites out of their loneliness, enthralled by their own embarrassment. I had been lonely myself, in the family sense; but I preferred that to the conniving coercion I saw as the standard family currency amongst my friends.

I drove us down, in the old Mini my father had bought me, and she grinned, enjoying eggs and sausages in a transport café, saying, "You're completely mad. He's a gorgeous old chap. Not so old, neither."

I said, "It's not so simple. Anyway, you needn't worry about it, need you? It's all to do with a will."

"Great," she said. "Go on. I love stories."

I was at a loss. I don't think anyone knew the full account, the voices, the house, the will, the station; O'Cleary, Father; I don't think I had it all, at that point, quite within my grasp; and what anyone else might have thought of it all didn't bear thinking about. I said, after a time, "I will tell you. At some point. If you're still interested by then," and she finished her mug of tea and said, "Oh, Tom. I expect I will be."

I was a free man, then, of course; no more forged notes and vivid excuses; I could pass any weekend I pleased with O'Cleary and Jenny who, at twenty, had drawn her whole life into a beautiful, artificial point. She had discarded her parents as if they were last year's clothes – living somewhere usefully folded, but neglected, and fading gently in the sunshine of a bedroom window. O'Cleary was her family, now; he called her "Little Squit", and "The Mistress", and I thought he was like a father to both of us. He had grown no older in the six years I had known him; he still squinted, quizzical, as he had the first time I'd seen him in Mrs. Jeffry's kitchen; the face-lines which should have aged him still made him look younger, instead.

I didn't much care for university; it was just a continuation of school; I felt no particular novelty about being on my own. I missed lectures and tutorials, shunting off to O'Cleary's lodge, hoping to find Jenny there, too; now, from Exeter, it wasn't such a long drive. Then there was Sally, of course; we began living together in a tiny flat, after a while; she began to wonder where I kept disappearing to. Because, for some reason, I didn't seem to want to bring them together. I didn't want to know what Jenny thought of Sally, or vice-versa. I couldn't imagine that it would be helpful.

What I did, in fact, was to take Sally to the little town, with the lodge, and the old house, the fun-fair and the pier, without telling her anything about it. It was late spring; I particularly enjoyed going there, then, driving down the steep hill road, looking at the one or two souvenir shops, which were still closed. Sally said, "Oh. This is pretty. Have you been here before?" and I made some sort of non-committal sound and drew off the promenade road, into the car-park which was only forty yards from Doctor Lister's house.

"You have," Sally said. "You've been here before. What are we doing here?"

I said, "I told you. Dirty weekend," but it didn't work. Jokes rarely worked for me; especially vulgar ones. She just looked at me; her small eyes narrowed; she wore no make-up that I could see. She said, "Well. You're up to something. I don't care. What are we doing now?"

We left the car, and stepped down onto the empty beach. Sally took her shoes off but I plodded on, feeling awkward, my feet holding pockets of silky sand. It seemed ridiculous to be there fully clothed, especially on such a warm day; but after a while, a breeze sorted itself out of the dunes, and my ears began to buffet as we trudged along towards the old pier.

"Oh, look," she said. "A pier!" and we stopped and sat in the sand and looked at it. She said, after a while, "That looks dangerous," and indeed it did. The supports were so tenuous by now that the whole thing was almost whipping itself about, and bits of it protruded, spars of wood at any angle like bristles. I said, "Yes, it is. I've been up on there," and we kissed each other in Sally's clean, defined way. "Good," she said. "Well. I suppose you're going to tell me about it, then," and, after a time, lying there on the sands, with her cruxed in my arm, I did.

I told it as an incident, an escapade; I didn't add that I still saw Jenny whenever she would let me; that, as far as I could tell, I always would. Sally said, "Silly bitch," and I couldn't argue with that, and we collected ourselves, knocking the sand off, walking towards and then past the pier. The barrier around its base had grown, to include dozens of solid-looking lumps of black, wet wood which had fallen within it. Sally said, "Oh dear. Looks like a bomb-site," and it did, with the barbed-wire and the grey, filthy sand, the teeth of old wood embedded everywhere. We left it, climbing up through the dunes; and there was Mrs. Jeffry's old house, the spring sun giving a pale shapeliness to the bricks, the willow and the crab-apple tree tidy and moulded in the back garden.

We cut through, climbed a steep little bank, and then we were on the rowan avenue, Sally saying, "What fantastic trees!" I had taken the big house for the weekend; it was easy to do, in those days; a local agent arranged the lettings. I had planned for weeks to bring Sally there, though heavens knows why; I suppose I wanted to see what she made of it. Perhaps I wanted to see it all through some fresh eyes. An intricate game, it was going to be, though at least there would be no Jenny or O'Cleary, to complicate it further. They were not due, then; I had made sure of that.

A small, fat woman answered the door. "Mr. Fellows," she said, not by way of a question. "I have your key here, and I'll just show you around the place." She worked for the agent.

I said, "Yes, thank you," and she led me into the kitchen, saying, "Kitchen," while Sally, said, "Oh, this is fine," and I thought of my father, solemn at the table, telling me about babies, the kitchen poised around him. Sally said, "It's fine, isn't it, Tom?" and I said yes, it was fine, and we went through into what the little woman called the lounge.

I said, "Oh. Where's . . .?" because the billiard table had gone; I hadn't been in the house for five years. Sally said, "What . . .?" and the woman said, "Oh, there's a loo downstairs, and a big bathroom up," so I said, "Thank you," and she led us upstairs.

I suppose that, in a sense, this story is about ghosts. In any case, I know that I felt like a ghost myself, that afternoon, haunting the old house, seeing it with thin, dry eyes, estranged and detached, as Mrs. Jeffry must have seen me in the station. I felt insubstantial on the stairs and, when the fat woman showed me into my old bedroom – a tiny, thin, spare bedroom which, she said, we wouldn't really be needing – my voice sounded like a rigid message from somewhere else. They went off, to see the bigger rooms, and I stood on my own for a few seconds, close to the door, standing where that other voice had inhabited, asking me about the future – when, in all fairness, it should have known as much about the future as anyone. I could see the rowans, out through the window, though there were no berries then, of course. The wind had finally gathered itself, the trees were bending; I looked suddenly to the window-sill, but there was no cocoa-tin.

The woman from the agent came back, and said, "Yes, it's a nice view, from here," and down we went. When she'd gone, Sally said, "Look at those trees. Let's go down. There's like a track," and off we went, the afternoon evolving more and more quickly, a wash glistening on the hedge. We could see the lodge and it was, indeed, empty: O'Cleary had business elsewhere, that weekend; he'd told me. I said, "I think this avenue only goes to that lodge. Let's have a look round at the garden."

Sally said, "Lodge? Oh. Yes. I suppose it is a sort of lodge. All right," and I led her back. We moved around the big house, dipping onto the rear lawn.

"There's a lake, back here, apparently," I said. "So I believe," and then Sally laughed.

"Good God," she said, good-naturedly. "A lake? Who told you that?"

I had to laugh, as well. We wandered together, up the slight mound, with the air-raid shelter entrance, giggling at the lake, which was a pond about six yards across. Once I had taken a strangely brittle walk across it, buoyed by a sort of moonlit mania; I sat there, seeking my own ghost, walking the water, expecting to see the thin boy, creeping, and looking back up at me.

I said, my voice separate in the air, "I'm sorry. They said a lake. The agents. If you don't like it . . ."

She said, "It's fine. It'll do. Don't fret," reassuring me, as people always did. Her shoulder-bone was on my side; she was very thin; Jenny, on the other hand, was slim. Slim and straight, with just enough plastic flesh on her to round the tiniest of bones; just enough to tuck finger-tips into, to dent slightly, like carpet. I loved Sally; we both knew we were going to get married, though we hadn't discussed it; but I could never be entirely without the whispered give of Jenny's arm.

The evening hung about in the sky for a time, then nipped down on us, coating the dusty interior with an emulsion of shades. The house grew back into itself; the sparse, cheap furniture which the agents had put in widened out again, the shadows spread themselves comfortably; I lit a fire. I wanted to take Sally to a hotel to eat, but she said, "Don't be daft. You can't afford this, as it is," and set about preparing a meal for us. Jenny never cooked. It was not in the order of things for Jenny to cook. O'Cleary was good in the kitchen; he spent hours there, leaving Jenny and me alone in the sitting-room; he matched the rhythms of his cooking to the rhythms of our love. But Sally could cook; she already ran me, like a vocation; she served.

I cannot tell you how much I wanted to explain the whole thing to her. We sat there, in the fading kitchen, eating spaghetti bolognaise, and I wanted so much to explain to Sally that I had been cheated and deluded and haunted as well; that the air in that house was known to me, I'd breathed it before, sharing it with a slightly rancid dead woman who might have been there, wallowing like a hippo in the murky air; or who might not have been there at all. I wanted to tell Sally that the house was really, by rights, my own house; that, at any rate, I had once believed it so. It didn't much matter, at that time, what the answer was to all that; what mattered was the question itself; it seemed to make me separate. She looked hard at me, that evening; she knew something was up; she watched me watching the kitchen cupboards, thinking of my father's back as he packed the tennis racquets. She said, "Leave the washing-up," and we went to bed, so that she could shuffle her small body into the folds of mine, so that I became, oddly enough, a container for her, a second skin podded around her bones. "Good stuff," she said, after a time, and went to sleep, coiled honestly against the quilt.

Naturally, I woke up in the small hours; I had expected to; I'd half expected the old woman to have another go at me, after all those years. We were in my father's old bedroom; indeed, it had been used by my mother, too, at one time. I lay there, thinking of her, for once. My life seemed crammed with women; there seemed hardly room for my poor, dead, mother; I hardly ever gave her a thought. I tried to fix her face, then; I tried to have it there, still; but it wasn't coming, it eluded me, almost standing and then vanishing, like an irritating insect. She'd had a flat forehead; her eyes had been wide apart; I knew this, but not from memory. It was like working on an artist's impression, building up an identi-kit with pieces of disjointed evidence. All I could do was compare: Mother, Mrs. Jeffry, Jenny, Joyce, Sally . . . So few men, it occurred to me; but, then, I didn't mind that, over much. Sally snored, slightly, contentedly; a small animal, nested, rested. Women were all right; and, of course, O'Cleary was as good as two or three other men put together.

The sky was brilliant, at breakfast; the cheap pots on the kitchen table glistened; each had a gleaming outline, and the sounds of plates and forks were small, defined. Sally moved between the cooker and the table with the same, small definition, in her boy's pyjamas. We would spend the day on the beach: the weather was better than we could have expected. "Come on," she said, sitting opposite me, spreading some marmalade that we'd found. "Tell me about it."

I said, "What?" I really didn't have any idea what she meant.

"This little lot," she said. "What's the story? I told you before: I love stories."

For some people, perception is just a habit, almost a physical bearing; you sense it in the way they walk, the way they bend in to you as they listen; there is a selective sharpness in the voice. It occurred to me that of all my roll-call of women, this girl was someone I'd met only weeks ago; she had somehow allocated herself to my life, integrated herself into my mornings with no particular effort on her part or mine. She seemed somehow to have been there always. Whereas with Jenny, of course, every time was the first . . .

"What do you mean?" I said. "What story?"

"Well, now," she said, a gentle mock in her voice, the joy of a little jibe. "'Lodge . . . Avenue . . . Lake . . .' What's all that, then? 'Avenue!' Family words, Thomas. Family words."

I think I actually blushed. She was right, of course; we'd called the track an "avenue"; the little cottage at the end of it, we'd named the "lodge". All families have their own codes; I'd heard them on the beach; sometimes, especially with the bigger families, you could hardly tell what they were talking about. Richard and Clem, my brothers, were quite good at it, but they never included me.

Anyway, "lodge" and the rest of them had been my father's words and, in a sense, they were a give-away; they had come too easily to me, the day before. So I said, "Yes. Well. We did holiday here, a few times," and Sally laughed, and started singing, "Tell us a story! Tell us a story!"

I watched her, and I said, "Right. All right. I'll tell you. Down on the beach. Let's go down on the beach." I didn't particularly like the sea, as I've said; but it seemed the right place to go.

We didn't walk over what I'd used to call the "field"; we were adults; we walked over the promenade, along the seafront, where the guest-houses were now called hotels, though most of them were still closed until July. There weren't many people about; but I recognised one figure, in an unnecessary overcoat, a short, polished man, hurrying along the pavement, looking confident in the wind. As he passed, I said, "Hello, Doctor Lister!" and he looked at me with the complete unfamiliarity of the professional man and said, "Oh. Yes. Good morning!", walking on; finding me, and the wind, and the grey sea, interesting.

Sally said, "My God. Who was that?"

"Oh," I said. "Just my psychiatrist," and she started laughing again; then, she stopped, and said, "Oh. I see."

"It's all right," I said. "I had a nervous breakdown, once. When I was twelve."

She said nothing; perhaps she was embarrassed; nervous breakdowns weren't so fashionable then as they are now. The sleek smell of frying onions was clinging to the air; we were passing the hot-dog-man; he was always there, on-season or off.

Sally sniffed, and said, "Mmm. Good stuff," and bought some, even though we'd just finished breakfast. She could eat anything, without becoming fat. So could Jenny, I imagine, but Jenny always refused, glancing in, at her own, immaculate body, perching herself artfully on the air, turning a landscape into a background. "No," she would say; onions or ketchup would have contaminated her. At fourteen, she had been, I suppose, a minx; at seventeen, she had driven herself in and out of my life with vigour and indifference; by now, at twenty, she had streamlined herself into a single, absorbing project: the creation of Jenny. She had grown taller, and become exquisitely beautiful.

A foot taller, she must have been, than Sally, who dropped mustard onto her chin, and sat down on a bench on the promenade. If she had been plumper, it occurred to me, she would have been almost cute; but the thinness gave her a serious line, even when she was laughing.

She said, "Come on, then, tell me the story of your life," and I did; I told her everything – except that Jenny was still important to me, that I still needed her to put me in my sweet place. I told her the lot; about half an hour, it must have taken; not much for a quarter of a lifetime, with two deaths, one affair, and one haunting. At the end of it, I said, "Well. What do you think of that?" and she paused, and said, "Well. I don't know. Let me think," screwing up the hot-dog wrapper, looking round for a waste-paper basket.

"It's a mug's game," the hot-dog-man said, when I was eight, learning to swim. I had looked at a girl in a bikini; the next day, we had tried the swimming again, but it hadn't worked; it still hasn't. I still can't do it; I still can't see a way to insert myself into the closing water, turning the world through ninety degrees, things taking place sideways. Nor do I particularly want to, to make a pleasure out of being out of control. Mrs. Jeffry had said, after two days of it, "You're useless, boy. You'll never get the hang of it," and, fussily, she had packed us off to the pictures, instead. I think it was a Norman Wisdom; she liked him; I think that, as far as I can remember, it was about Norman Wisdom trying to become a singer. He kept asking fat people to help him; he kept on being unimportant; girls, nevertheless, kept on falling in love with him. Mrs. Jeffry laughed; she was, I think, relieved to be out of the water although, to me, it didn't seem much better. Norman Wisdom was very boring; I couldn't see why she liked him, so much, and yet disliked me; we seemed so much the same.

After the film, she took me up onto the pier; it was good and safe and solid, then. I was pleased; I nagged incessantly for the pier; I liked the slot machines. I careered about on it, liking the hollow sound of my feet, slapping myself all over it. I wasn't much interested by the sea, walloping about below; I wasn't impressed by its mystery; what I liked, when I was eight, was getting a prize every time. I would squeeze sixpence out of Mrs. Jeffry, then squeeze it back into a glass-topped machine, converting a bit of every-day life into something worth having. On that day, after the Norman Wisdom, I remember that the machine was a chick. A small, rough chicken, with a mechanical mouth, turning in jerky circles above a mess of earrings and bubblegum. I watched it move, juddering and jarring about like a piece of cheese on a wire; then it sorted out a tiny thing for me, and chucked it down the chute.

It was a little skeleton, the size of my thumb, pliable as a leaf; a central bone of white plastic, ribbed all the way down with white feathers, bending, like a feather itself. It coiled itself any way at all; the backbone was anybody's; it would contort with elegant acquiescence, humbling itself in my pocket. On top was a tiny, flat skull; the arms ended in grasping sticks. "Look," I said to Mrs. Jeffry. "It looks like Norman!" but she only thought I was being rude, in some way, and we banged off the pier, back to the big house, back to the little bedroom which the fat lady from the agent had said I would never really need.

I left it a few minutes, but she was obviously preoccupied, her legs stuck out to their small length in front of the bench. After a while, I said, again, "What do you think?" but she only said, "I'm trying to work it out; it's interesting," which annoyed me slightly, because she sounded like Doctor Lister; things are only interesting when they're not very important. The sea looked like an oyster-shell, whorled and static; there were never any ships; nor, in those days, did people do things like wind-surfing. I looked at her, and then we stood up and walked down to the pier, so that I could propose to her which, as we both understood, was one of the points of the excursion.

The pier stood over us, as I did it; I suppose that I should say that it stood there like an altar; but it didn't. It simply boxed us in in a loose, erratic kind of way as I suggested to Sally that, since we were already living together, in our student flat, in the middle of Exeter, we might as well get married.

Sally said she thought it was a good idea. It wasn't a

romantic scene, though the love was there, all right, breaking on our faces like spring sunshine, important and predictable. She said that we should get a better flat, if we could afford it; ours was too small; it inhibited us. So did the business with Jenny, she added. That needed to be sorted out, too.

Well; I was slightly surprised. I hadn't actually indicated that there remained any business with Jenny to sort out at all; but Sally was too clever for that. She thought that it would be helpful if Jenny and she met. I didn't, of course; I could imagine nothing more appalling; but there was nothing to be said.

At that time, life seemed like a maze. Sally didn't understand it, any more than I did; but she wasn't in it, with me. She could look in, as it were, from above, and see me fumbling about. Occasionally, she would lean in towards me with the odd direction.

So, when she said, "Yes. I think I want to see the wonderful Jennifer," I said, "Yes. Of course. I'll try to arrange it. It'll be in that little house," I added. "Probably."

"Yes," said Sally. "I see. The lodge," and, for some reason we were laughing again, and we left the beach, climbing up the small bank, to the house, and to bed.

13

Toby lasted about a year. I called him "Toby"; Father called him "King", and glared at me; I gather that his mother had had a dog with that name. I was only about ten, but even then it struck me that Father's behaviour was absurd. Perhaps the rift between us opened up then; we started looking at each other's foreheads in conversations. After a year or so, Toby just wandered off; I didn't particularly mind. He was a tedious little dog and every time I looked at him, I thought of the names, the problems, and Jenny's ability to sort the world.

In the spring of 1968, I proposed to Sally, and I went up to Birmingham to tell Father. I think that he'd retired, by then; certainly he was at home, during the day, during the week; he was lying in bed in the afternoon, gaunt and long.

He got up, though, when I arrived; he came down to the sitting-room, where the housekeeper, Mrs. Malpass, had laid out the daily papers – the *Mail*, the *Mirror* – as if it were a hotel, a genteel lounge, off-season. She was like a ghost, too; she had distilled discretion into an aching sort of non-presence; Father used to write her notes. She had her own ways, though; the sitting-room had grown angular under her regime; Joyce called her "Mrs. Impasssse".

She showed me in; she seemed to apologise for her presence; her head seemed unable to move on her neck. I felt embarrrassed for her. Then Father came in, ekeing out a sort of geometry, his eyes red-mad. It was only weeks since I'd seen him, fawning over Sally; I had no idea that he was so ill.

Mrs. Malpass said that she would make tea, but Father found some sherry, so that, when she reappeared with the unwanted apparatus, set out like chintz chess, she could allow her mouth a little pivot of distaste, her eyes a little, painful search at the window. I don't know where Father got these women from.

Anyway, we sat in the bay window; I glanced through it; it was a dull day; engagements and weddings seemed better suited to sunshine, the June air hanging on a beach, than to drizzle in a Birmingham suburb, the walls black with wet. I looked at the wall, about three houses up, where I had sat, years ago, wondering where I lived.

I said, "Well. If you don't mind. That's what we want to do. I hope you're pleased." Technically, I was seeking his permission, though I was certain he wouldn't object to anything I did. He seemed preoccupied, nevertheless; he reminded me fleetingly of Mrs. Jeffry, in her last days; absorbed by his own illness.

It was difficult to say, "You don't look well, Father," because we weren't close enough; we had only ever been polite. I asked him how he was a number of times, instead, but he didn't answer; he remarked once that Mrs. Malpass did a good job.

She stood in a corner of the kitchen, wishing herself not there; I wondered, briefly, where she would wish to be, instead. She had appeared after my time, as it were; I'd never really had a conversation with her.

I had to have one now, though. "What's wrong with him?" I asked, and she put down her own coffee; she mustn't drink in my presence; we both watched it going cold.

"It's all right," she said. "The doctor comes in, on a Wednesday. He's to take it easy, that's all."

Through the tall, sash windows, spring was blurring the garden, making a mess of the forsythia. "Yes," I said. "Good. But what's actually the matter?"

She said, "Oh, nothing you can name. He can't put his finger on it. He hasn't had a heart attack, or anything," she added, and I admired her for that, at any rate.

"He's too much on his own," she added; the neck moved, stretched, duck-like, in a tiny, silent tut.

She meant that I neglected him; but I didn't feel too guilty about that. I came home more often than the others; I only saw them at Christmas, nowadays; and, after all, my relationship with Father was worse than theirs. The fact that I had spent the last five or six years ignoring, avoiding, disobeying and deceiving him seemed to me then as much his fault as it was mine. "There is no fault; there is only circumstance", somebody had been quoted as saying, by a teacher at school, in English Literature. Father was part of my circumstance.

Nevertheless, ordinary decency propelled me back into some sort of equanimity, and I chatted to him, all afternoon, about Exeter, and about Latin; he was, in some ways, quite a learned man, though he displayed it in aphorisms, in anecdotes. After a couple more sherries, he was in full flow. "The Romans," he was saying, "were a people of motivation. Take the Latin," he went on, "for 'in order to'. The Latin for 'in order to' is 'ut'. 'Ut'," he repeated. "Purpose to the Romans was as instinctive as a grunt." I suppose it was reasonable, after-dinner stuff, for some circles, but I was bored out of my mind. I was bored, I reflected, as I listened, for most of the time. Latin bored me solid – which, I think, was why I'd chosen it.

The rain gave up on the Sunday and, suffused with a kind of mild, alcoholic benignity, I got Father out into a garden seat so that he could watch me greasing the lawn-mower. He had been an adequate gardener, at one time, but now I noticed that the grass had resorted to clumps and some thistles were spreading, flat and exotic, like spider-webs. "I'll get up again, soon," I said. "Give you a hand with this lot," because, after all, the past was the past and he was just an old man, suddenly, framed in the french window, in the patio and in the decent square of town garden. I slicked my fingers into the grease-tin; soon, I would try to start the thing, wrenching at the rope with a strange, mechanical fury. It was an annual ritual.

★ ★ ★

"I've got to work it out," Sally had said; her openness of mind was tougher than other people's prejudice. She had sat me down, on a Sunday evening, a few weeks before, and we had worked our ways through the entire incidence of my haunting. It was so simple; to turn the thing into a list; to convert the dim circles of recollection into linear avenues, each memory straight and separate; explicable, normal, like a tree.

"First time, then," she had said, sitting on the thin armchair; it was our second and last night in Mrs. Jeffry's big house.

"Right," I said, as she wrote carefully in her notebook – so unlike Doctor Lister. "Right. That was – you know. The night she died. 'What happens now?' That was the first."

"O.K.," she said. "Yes. So. We can put that down, then, to your being, shall we say, worked up. This Jenny thing. I mean, that was the first time anything like that . . ."

I said, "Yes. Sexual excitement and frustration," and she laughed.

"My God," she said. "The way you speak!" But she wrote it down; she had columns; one for the incident, one for our explanation. All we had to do was complete both columns. It was like being back at school – except for the warm intensity at the back of my neck.

She went on; a strange, methodical exorcism, it was, as the night grew rich around us. "Second time," she said and I said, "Next morning, then. That's the one, really. About the will."

"Yes," she said. She looked at me carefully, for a few seconds; then she said, "Have you never . . . Has nobody ever done this before, with you?"

It is remarkable, to hold a secret for so many years. Only Jenny knew about any of it, and for her, it was merely an entertainment – like everything else.

"Well," I said. "No. Actually," and I started to cry; it was a release, all right.

"Now," she said, a little later, "what you've got to do is, work out whether she, you know, ever said anything to you at all, when she was alive, I mean, anything at all that could have led you to dream, or imagine, you know, that she was going to put you in her will. Even if you were wrong."

I sat, and thought, and said, "No," and thought some more; we had to fill the second column. "What I'm trying to do," she said, "is to find a rational explanation for each one. You could easily have imagined this, but it'd be helpful if we could account for why, exactly."

Then, it came to me: a phrase she used to use; I suppose it could have been sitting, fermenting, in my head. "Yes," I said to Sally. "She used to say, 'I'll see you right.' She used to say that I'd be surprised, one day," and I was seeing her tight face, sherry carried on the air. "I didn't understand what she meant. She was drunk, half the time."

"Right." Sally was writing, again. "Yes. Well. She probably meant nothing much; but it could have been enough to make you dream up this, about the legacy. Couldn't it?"

It was with immense relief that I reflected that it could: I thought about it again, as I yanked at the mower and the mower shuddered and refused to live. Father sipped a sherry; he seemed to drink more than he'd used to; I couldn't see why he shouldn't.

"Yes," said Sally. "But the whole sick-bay thing is easy. You were upset, in disgrace. Anyway, you were an adolescent, in a boarding school. And, you know, you were having a nervous breakdown, at the time. Well, Tom, you were. There's no point beating about the bush. You couldn't even find your own house. You didn't know whether your Father had a moustache or not. It's not surprising if you had fantasies."

I drank some beer, from a can, and looked at the rectangle of space where the billiard-table had been. It was possible that I could think, "Poor old Father," thinking of my suspicions, of his pliant back, when, perhaps, I had made up the whole thing myself.

"All right," I said. "What about what she actually said, though?" For years, it had puzzled me that the dead woman had been so inconsistent, especially in her attitude to Jenny, ranging from condemnation and warning to approval and encouragement. I explained it, to Sally. "She started by calling her a bitch," I said. "But then later, she told me to go to her." 'She will lift you into all happiness': I was remembering the distant, dead poetry with its odd, physical accuracy.

"Yes," said Sally. "And I bet you went, as well." There was silence for a few seconds; we both sensed the turn of Jenny's neck, I think; in our different ways, we both scented her silk blouse.

I said, "I'm sorry," and Sally said, "Don't be daft. Anyway," she added, "It's O.K., because it fits, perfectly. What you heard was just yourself. You know. Desire. Guilt. It's obvious. Really."

She was tidying up her notes; I said, "What about the railway station, then? I actually saw her," but I already knew the answer; I was defeated, relieved and confused. "You were tired; frustrated, dozing. Just a dream, Thomas, my lad. Just a dream. Come on now," and she stood up, stretching in her compact, organised way. "Come and dream some more."

I thought I heard a telephone; but, at that moment, the mower exploded into aggressive life; Father nearly dropped his sherry. Standing there, with the thing working, the grass tickling my ankles, I had no choice; I shouted, "I'll just give it a go, then!" and let it run me around the lawn. After a minute or two, the sun went; the light simply dropped, as it can in June; I glanced up to see Mrs. Malpass helping Father into the house. I could tell from the angle of her arm that I should have been doing that.

Mrs. Malpass served us dinner; it was surprisingly good; home-made soup and then roast pork. I made a particular effort; Father looked better and better; the white stretch went out of his skin; his eyes dimmed. I made some jokes, but it was an uncomfortable meal, because Mrs. Malpass sat with us, an honour which she clearly hated. She made her corner of the table into a separate, parenthetical decoy; and she kept on having to get up and clear away, so that I felt awkward not helping her; but, nevertheless, Father seemed immensely cheered. I said, "I've got to be off first thing. I won't wake you. But I'll be back, probably the weekend after next. I'll bring Sally, if that's all right."

Mrs. Malpass said, "If you could let us know, I could make up the attic bedroom for your young lady," and I said, beaming, "That's all right, Mrs. Malpass. She sleeps with me," and Father nearly choked with good humour; for the first time ever, or so it seemed, we were sharing a joke. Mrs. Malpass said, "Well, I'll take my coffee in the kitchen. Get started on the clearing up," and Father laughed again.

"Awful woman," he said. "But, after all, very efficient. Very efficient." He was still laughing when the phone rang.

I answered it; it was in the cold hall, near the front door. Sally's voice said, "Oh. At last. I've been trying you all afternoon."

I said, "What's up?" We had no arrangement for such a call.

"Well," she said. "No, it's not a problem. It's just you've had this letter. Recorded delivery. So I thought I'd better open it. Then I thought I'd better ring you . . ."

I could hear the rustle of paper. "Well?" I said. "Go on."

She said, "It's – um – it's from some solicitors. Purbright's, apparently. Jermyn Street. It – oh, look, I'll just read it out, O.K.?"

Father's house had a massive hall; the staircase rose and turned from it; every line was emphasised with picture-rails, banisters, cornices. It was unheated; cold even in early summer; and I think I shivered with apprehension, too, because, somehow, I knew what was coming.

I could already see the argument; I couldn't keep the bitterness out of my mouth; it was behind my teeth; as strong a feeling as I sometimes felt when Jenny, as she sometimes did, closed her bedroom door in my face, to sleep alone, because I'd annoyed her.

There was silence in the phone; I hadn't answered. I had so much wanted to go back into the dining-room, smiling at Father, who was stretched across his chair like a dust-sheet. I had so much wanted to work the repair, now that I was getting married, and he was getting ill; but, even before she read it to me, I knew that the letter had put a stop to that. I could see the argument set out already, a little agenda of distrust; because the lie had been there all along.

It seemed sad but predictable that it would have to intrude then, at the moment when I had thought I'd been laying it, like a ghost. Just when Father had become too old and strained to take it; just at the moment of the parching of his body, the drying of his intellect, I was going to have to have it out with him. After six years.

I said to Sally, wearily, "All right. Go on, then," and she did.

"It says: 'As executor of the above-named estate' – that's, you know, the old woman – 'I am required on the occasion of your majority to inform you that you are named as principal beneficiary in the testament of Mrs. Louisa Magdalen Jeffry, deceased . . .' Blah blah . . . They want you to go and talk to them. You know. At your convenience. That's it." She waited; I waited, too; perhaps Mrs. Jeffry was there, waiting with us; I don't know what for.

After a time, I put the phone down, and I went upstairs, to my old bedroom, Mrs. Jeffry's old bedroom, with the massive television-set. She had lost herself in the deep, green screen; she had swum in it, like a shadowy fish, cavorting with Elsie Tanner and Len Fairclough; she had launched herself from the pouffe into a separate, elegant oblivion. I realised then that she had drawn things out of it, too; she had taken Father, and Jenny, and O'Cleary, and me; she had made us into her favourite programme; the will had been the script. And, all along, her name had been Louisa. A southern name; the name of some blue flower; I couldn't see that it could be hers, as well.

I sat, on the edge of the bed, for some minutes. I tried to think of Father's deception. I tried to think of the old woman's manipulation, her creation of my life simply for her own diversion. I tried to think of being rich – for, certainly, she had been a very wealthy woman. I tried to be angry, or confused, or even elated. But all I could manage was the name. "Louisa," I said, quietly. It was like a whisper; a young woman's name; though perhaps it would do well enough, after all, for a ghost.

My only case was on the bed, and I took it, creeping downstairs. Mrs. Malpass was audible in the kitchen; in the dining-room, Father was, I think, talking quietly to himself. I left them; the row was not to be; within half an hour I was on the A.38, bouncing, very fast, towards the West Country. I thought I was going to Sally; I didn't pay much attention; only when I was stopped by a policeman and asked where I was going to, in such a hurry, did I realise that it was O'Cleary, after all, who was waiting; O'Cleary and Jenny whom I needed to lift me out and console me in their own, separate ways.

14

Sally's father gave her away. He murmured to me, in the church, in the service itself: "It's O.K." He meant that he was pleased.

The congregation perched on the pews, divided like football supporters. Sally's parents and cousins topped up one side of the church; the brothers and others sat conspicuously on the other; Jenny was there, too, in a blue dress. The aisle was the thin line where the families joined; that was our job; we bagged the aisle for ourselves, the pivots of the ritual.

I held up a book – the order of service; I remember the vicar moving it, so that Sally could see it, too; we had to share. It was like school; you had to share, and you had to say what the others said, your voice disappearing above you, the echo lending it a spurious dignity, the sound crawling over stone.

I said that I did take her under the conditions set down in front of me by the vicar. As I've said before, I didn't much believe in any of it; but I was pleased to think of Mrs. Jeffry watching; I felt protected from her, in there; protected by the solid walls, and by Sally herself, whose hair was so severe that she looked like an aggressive page-boy.

I was happy, all right, but also mildly irritated by all the questions. It seemed obvious that, if the answers to any of them had been "no", I wouldn't have been there in the first place. Then again, I think I was lying, some of the time. I didn't actually chant to the effect of not going to bed with Jenny, ever again; I didn't slide such a promise into the horizontal sunshine; if I had done, it wouldn't have been true.

There was a fine window, behind the vicar, and I watched that, for most of the time. It was full of colossal robes, breaking each other in a sort of crystal flow; and the whole lot worked against a thick frame of black, lead squares, as if they were all caught in a net. The vicar asked me if I would do certain things. I said I would. Behind me, Sally's father muttered his approval, his reassurance. Behind him, Jenny stood; I imagined her, yawning slightly, behind a blue-gloved hand. O'Cleary hadn't come.

Three months earlier, at about one-thirty in the morning, a policeman on a motorcycle had stopped me, just outside Taunton. "You're in a great hurry," he said; his voice was not unkind. "Where are you off to, then?"

I opened my mouth, to say "Exeter," but another word came out, instead, and I realised that I was going to a little seaside town, a town with a fair and a pier. The constable said, "Well. Just you take it easy, then," and I was off again, completing the journey as I had begun it, six hours before: entirely without control or purpose.

My head began to clear as I drove down the hill, into town; I began to wonder what to do. I really hadn't had a single, coherent thought, before then; for six hours or more I had simply watched the windscreen wipers segmenting and re-segmenting the sparkling darkness.

But now it began to occur to me that O'Cleary might not be at home; he was often away; and Jenny certainly wouldn't be there; she only appeared when I was promised, and they weren't expecting me. Still, I had my key. Even if he wasn't there, to joke me out of it, then at least I could spend a day or two there in peace.

It was a clear June night; I parked the car and, above me, the sky receded; centuries of darkness. I watched it, for a time; I tried to see some constellations; then I looked down at the sea. Once again, I was having some sort of undefined crisis. I couldn't tell whether it was a catastrophe. I seemed to have discovered that the ghost was true, after all; Sally's careful columns hadn't seen it off; perhaps it was on my shoulder at that minute, deft, familiar, sleek. I thought of Mrs. Jeffry beside me, always: beside me in bed; caressing Jenny, perhaps, as I caressed; stroking us both. I thought of her beside me in the silent car, on the promenade; I thought of her with every relaxing creak of the engine.

Had she eavesdropped as I proposed to Sally? Had she giggled, girlishly, as Sally ticked her off in a notebook? Would she make a sprightly dance of it, expertly footing up the aisle, kicking her dead, dancing boots behind us? I tried to see her, again, as I had seen her on the station, her old skirt rubbing on her dirty legs; I tried to catch the hairs on her upper lip, to sense the rustle of her thought, the tiny odour of chrysanthemum in the waiting-room. I tried to see her in front of me now, folding herself in and out of the black, glittering water, resting, like a seal, on its giving surface. It seemed necessary, now, that she had been there always: my one, true, constant companion.

O'Cleary's door always whined; I let myself in as quietly as I could. It was about half-past two and, if he were there, I didn't want to wake him. Father was a liar; I was haunted; there was nothing particularly new, after all, about any of it; perhaps, in time, I would begin to feel reasonably happy. I was, presumably, about to become rich; Mrs Jeffry hadn't actually appeared for years; perhaps she was playing with somebody else, now. It was a strange kind of limbo to be in: to be sitting in someone else's sitting-room; haunting, as it were, the edge of someone else's life, and wondering how I was going to feel in the morning.

It is often true that a long drive isn't conducive to sleep. I sat in the semi-darkness; the moon was nearly full; its light hit the tiles of the fireplace, scattering in shards through the still room. I thought again of the old ghost; and it occurred to me, quite suddenly, that if Mrs. Jeffry were still floating about in her aimless suspension, then presumably others were, too; there was something like it for all of us; the air was crammed with spirits, stiff with corpses, writhing like eels. I had once, in a market up the coast, seen a wheelbarrow full of spider-crabs: there must have been fifty of them, thrown in there, all over the place; on their backs, their ends, their heads. But they were all quite alive; alive, when they should surely have been dead; alive, with their red eyes fixed on a horizon of claws and backs; crawling with immense, shuddering effort over a landscape of crawling, falling spider-crabs; evolving themselves, around and around, dogged, determined pointless. Sitting in O'Cleary's empty house, feeling the vacant air around me, loose air hanging like a shroud, it occurred to me that that memory of spider-crabs might be an image of the spirits all around me, pursuing themselves through days and nights, searching for an edge.

I have to say that, despite the nature of this story, I have never been noticeably nervous about the supernatural. Even when convinced that I had become the object of a decrepit old ghost's interest, I had rarely been actually frightened. But I must add that this sudden, crowded vision did begin to seep through me, subtly lightening my nerve-endings, so that gravity seemed to elude my hands and feet and stomach. I began to hear noises; all old houses hinge themselves about, at night; O'Cleary's walls rubbed and kissed the oak beams with soft, sucking noises; the occasional breeze folded over the little roof and worried the chimney; I suppose that I was very tired. Anyway, as I say, I began to hear noises.

It was a tiny, discreet, rhythmic noise; an ancient, almost subliminal rocking, eerily comforting, exactly on the edge of perception. It had nothing to do with Mrs. Jeffry, I knew that; and that made it more disturbing, because, over the years, she had become almost familiar. It seemed, when I could hear it at all, to be the sound of a footstep; a resolute, nagging footstep; a footstep in sand, dragging, of course; but growing closer. At first, a simple wince of the eye dispelled it; but after what must, I suppose, have been some ten minutes or so, its existence became just slightly established. Then there seemed the occasional voice; just the odd counterpoint. I sat, exactly still. The sound grew. Then it stopped. Then there was a single peal of laughter; totally abandoned. After that, I heard footsteps on the stair, and the sitting-room door opened, and Jenny came in, giggling, wearing no clothes at all, and shouting, "Just you wait! Just you wait!"

She looked at me, for some seconds; she put the light on; I could see the shock on her face – the last unrehearsed expression I was ever to see there. But she began to change it almost immediately; the eyes began to move down and in, the forehead to drop, the mouth to flatten out and, eventually, to start work on a smile. It was a remarkable process to watch; I could feel the effort of it; it was as plastic as if she were doing it with her hands, her fingers gouging and moulding the wax of the cheeks. What she ended up with was a look of premeditated evil.

And she knew how to stand, did Jenny; it was her life's work. Even in those circumstances, there was the imperceptible adjustment of the hip, the achievement of the diagonal, the hip squeezed into a small shelf, the tiny stomach aslant, one bare foot arched. I had found her in bed with another man, but it was suddenly I who felt guilty, awkward and lost; I it was who was the intruder; separate, once again.

O'Cleary's voice was continuing in the background, yelling, laughing, commanding. She called up, once, "Tom!" but that, of course, was ambiguous, and he carried on, oblivious after sex. After a time, Jenny turned and went, and then there was a period of silence so that I could reflect on what the spirit-noise had really been: a noise most certainly of this world, after all.

It always seems to me, when these things happen, that I'd known about it in advance; it had begun with my mother's death. Perhaps it's the same for everyone; I don't know. All of my life was being re-shuffled, at that point, but to me it was history already. Of course O'Cleary slept with Jenny: who wouldn't? I could see it already in my every recollection of the two of them together; a hand on a shoulder; an arm across a neck. I could sense it in the very smell of the lodge: it always had Jenny's perfume, even when she hadn't been there for weeks; O'Cleary and I had joked about that. Well; he'd been lying, then; they'd both been lying, and laughing at me, awaiting my visits with the double fun of irony. They were liars, but of course that didn't matter; I was quite a liar myself.

I could hear them moving about upstairs; clothes were being put on; some sort of conversation was to take place. I didn't want that; I think I was too tired and, anyway, I had to sort myself out, first. I crept upstairs, instead, to my own room; it occurred to me that I had quite a lot of bedrooms, all at the same time. This one, in the lodge, was the one where Jenny had lifted me, three years before, into a warm, ethereal suspension, her hands on my back. I had all night now to wonder what exactly she did for O'Cleary.

Oddly enough, that wasn't really the problem. It had been some years by then since I had actually liked my cousin; some years since I had wanted her company, other than for our essential transactions in bed. It was O'Cleary who had deserted me, it seemed; O'Cleary who had taken his turn again to be a liar, a false friend. I didn't cry, as I dropped off to sleep, finally; but if I had done, it would have been for him.

I dreamt of the egg, for the first time in years; it had become perfectly round, and packed tight with all sorts of people, journeying carefully around its insides. As I crawled, I saw Doctor Lister, worming along, with his glasses on; he was crawling over Father, whose body had grown long and curved, to match the egg-wall itself. Jenny and O'Cleary weren't there; perhaps they had escaped; but I saw Sally, at one point, her fingers slithering on the marble floor. There should have been a wailing, I suppose: the lost souls should have been mourning the deathly fatigue of immortality. But they weren't: the dream was completely silent, and slow, spinning like a planet out of the night.

I was late going down, in the morning: a hot, summer, seaside morning, with the tiny sound of the beach in the sitting-room window. O'Cleary was on the settee; he was in his dressing-gown, looking like the emperor of Ireland.

I had no idea at all of how we would approach each other. I

waited for him, and, with no pause at all, he got up, and said, "Tom." It wasn't a welcome; it wasn't an apology.

I said, "I'm sorry . . ." though I've no idea why. Jenny was moving about upstairs. I think I wanted to get out, go away; but that didn't seem possible, yet. The piece had its own rhythm.

Then Jenny came in. She was wearing baby-doll pyjamas: a tiny nightie, reaching to her navel, and a pair of pink briefs. My throat began to ache.

They both sat down again, side by side, on the settee, and Jenny said, "You've got a bit of a nerve."

I said, again, "I'm sorry . . ." but O'Cleary interrupted.

"No," he said. "No, Tom. Not fair. I'm sorry. I'm the one who's sorry." He looked into the empty fireplce; Jenny stirred restlessly, working her shoulders; she placed one leg carefully over O'Cleary's thigh, so that he could pat it.

"I'm sorry that we've had to do this, really," he went on, and I realised that it wasn't going to be quite the apology I'd expected. "Only, you see, you weren't going to have all that money. That was mine."

His voice was indifferent, vague, indolent. The Irish, which I liked so much, had almost entirely gone. Then he said, to Jenny, "Don't you think you'd better get dressed?"

She glanced at me, and moved the leg off O'Cleary, crossing it over the other one, very slowly. "Oh, I don't think so. Tom prefers me like this," she said, "don't you, Tom?"

"Yes," I said; though I knew that it was the wrong answer to an important question. I couldn't take my eyes off her; I wanted her more than ever.

I said, "Look. Can I get this right? What you're saying is, that all that's happened . . . me coming down here, all that . . . that's all been really because of the money. In some way?"

O'Cleary said, "Oh, yes, I'm afraid so . . ." and Jenny said, "Listen, idiot. She left the money to you. In trust until you came of age. Tom's been contesting it ever since. It's his money, not yours. He's her son." She kissed him, on the cheek, her mouth flattening out against him; and then she turned his face towards her, and kissed him on the mouth, for me to watch.

I stood up; there was, after all, Sally, somewhere; I should have gone to her in the first place. "No," said Jenny. "Sit down. I'll tell you about it."

So I did as I was told, and she explained to me how O'Cleary had got wind of his mother's death, and come for his legacy, to discover that I was named in the will. He'd taken various approaches to contesting it. At one time, he had hoped to prove me unfit to inherit; he'd hidden the egg-photograph, apparently, to help along my nervous breakdown; but I'd got better, all the same. The next plan was to allow me to have the money, after all, and to bleed me dry, through Jenny.

"That's what we were going to do," she explained. Even though the plan was now foiled, she took a feline pleasure in its detail; explaining it to me, as she coiled subserviently over O'Cleary, was part of her revenge.

"I was going to marry you," she said; she pouted slightly, though whether at her disappointment, or at the distasteful prospect of the marriage itself, I couldn't tell. "That's why we let you down here so often. I was going to marry you, and get the money, bit by bit, and give it to Tom." She kissed him again, and, partly just to stop that, I asked, "Why?"

She said, misunderstanding the question. "What do you mean? You know that if I asked you for anything, you'd give it to me. You know that, Tom. Remember? Anything at all . . ."

It was a game she used to play with me. She would take me into her bedroom, and say, "Now. What would you do, for me? Just to have the pleasure of me? For one night?"

It began harmlessly enough. I would say, "I'd rob a bank," or "I'd give you everything I own," but it became increasingly sinister, over the years. She would stand before me, saying, "No, Tom, you'll have to do better than that"; she would be toying with her underwear, her finger hooked in a strap. I had to make up wilder and wilder promises; they became increasingly desperate, violent, humiliating; up to now, I had taken it as an erotic game. Nothing, I began to realise, had been a game; nothing, in the last six years, had been spontaneous.

"Yes," I said. "But, I mean, why give it to O'Cleary? You'd have the money, anyway. What's he got to do with it?" I was crying, I noticed: voluminously.

O'Cleary smiled, and Jenny said, "Oh. Just because I do everything Tom tells me to do," and I could see that it was true; it was a kind of pure, sexual worship; the exact opposite of her relationship with me. "You'd better go, now," Jenny added. "Don't come down here again," and O'Cleary stretched on the settee, and smiled at me as I went.

Politely, she showed me to the door; the sun hit me, solid, when she opened it. I said, "Hang on." I felt immensely calm, again; confirming one's own unimportance is always relieving. "Hang on. Are you saying that there was an egg-photo, then. He hid it? Put another in its place?"

"Yes," she said. "Yes. That's right." She was thinking about it; it had been, after all, some years ago. "That's right," she repeated. "We were hoping to get you committed, at that point. He'd be next of kin, you see. We were trying to help you go mad." She grinned; it was as if we were talking about an innocent joke, played on someone else.

"I see," I said. "I suppose it would have been better for you if I'd just fallen off the pier, that night. Saved you a lot of trouble," and she said, vaguely, "What? Oh. Yes, I suppose so," but I could tell that she didn't know off-hand what I was talking about; she'd forgotten it all.

Strangely enough, it was that that upset me more than anything else.

15

Mr. Purbright said, "It was, originally, a simple matter." He had some sherry; he was enjoying himself immensely; it was as if the inheritance were actually his. I suppose it made a change from property disputes and divorces.

"But then," he went on, "Mr. Thomas O'Cleary arrived on the scene." He paused, as if for dramatic effect. No wonder Mrs. Jeffry had chosen him as her solicitor; he seemed to live, like her, in the world of television drama.

I must have looked a sight; perhaps that added to the frisson of the scene. Purbright's was in London, and I had driven there directly from O'Cleary's lodge, without wash, food or sleep, arriving in the late afternoon. London was sticky.

"Yes," I said. "I see."

"Oh, I doubt it, Mr. Fellows," he said, meaninglessly, "I doubt that very much. You see," he went on, after a waggish little curl of the lip, "the money was to be held in trust for you, in the terms of the will, until you came of age. Your father, as I imagine you know, by now, didn't want you to know about it, because Mr. – um – O'Cleary had a fair case for contestation, and it might have all come to nothing. Better for you not to know, of course. No false expectations!" It was a fair phrase, for him; he spoke like someone out of Dickens, though his office was modern and very bright.

"It was made all the more difficult, you see," he said; and he poured me some more sherry; I had thought that that only happened in films; "all the more – ah – difficult, at first, by the names. You see, she called you just 'Thomas'. No surname, you see. Mr. O'Cleary's name, too. He tried to base his claim on that, at first. But, of course, that fell through. Internal evidence. In fact, the whole of the contestation has been finally withdrawn. So now, in effect, the – er – whole thing is yours, as it were. Over to you."

He smiled, and sat back; he had a long, thin nose. "Oh," I said. "Well. What do I do now?"

"Ah," he said; he was suddenly serious. "You must see, that I am Mrs. Jeffry's solicitor, and executor, of course. I am not your solicitor, you see. I cannot advise you. But I can say to you informally that as I see it, there remains no problem with the bequest; that you fulfil the requirements, and that the signing of a series of documents should release to you the property, capital and bonds which in total, and even allowing for death duties, expenses and so on, will be worth about half a million pounds."

I said, after a pause, "Can it really take so long? She died when I was twelve," and he said, immediately, "Oh. Oh. Easily. Longer. Easily," and I was thinking of her, propped up in bed, the nose tilted like a beak as she told us about Norman Wisdom. "I could have wept," she'd said, but she hadn't: she'd laughed instead; and, in a few hours, she'd blinked and shrunk down into death, leaving me a fortune, in more senses than one.

Later on, I supposed, I would explain it to Sally; later than that, Father would explain it to me; but I didn't feel that I could stomach any of that. I'd had enough explanation, in the last twenty-four hours; I asked Mr. Purbright for some more sherry; I thought I'd probably wander into the West End and get drunk. After all, I seemed to have the money for it.

I don't know London at all. I've never been keen on cities; I suppose that that's what comes of being brought up in Birmingham. Exeter, really, is just a big village; I wasn't used to the constant pull of the traffic, the skyline pushed down to shop-front level; layer after layer of street. It was, I suppose, the prime time to see London; on a hot summer evening, in 1968, the air shaking with American voices. I wasn't much interested, at first; I noticed that you could buy an ice-cream for a pound, if you wanted to; I saw an open-top bus, bright red, like a film prop.

There was an elation. I don't know why; I suppose that the thought of the money helped; and the growing sense that at last things were getting sorted out; the friends and enemies were lining up, like the families in church. I could stand, after all, to be haunted; I'd stood it since I was twelve. Perhaps I'd feared some sort of dilemma; that, if it came to it, I would have to choose between the money and peace of mind. However, now that it had happened, there seemed no choice at all. I had few friends; I had a bitch for a mistress; I had a stranger for a father; but, on the other hand, I had Sally; and I had a very great deal of money. I cannot believe anyone who says that having a great deal of money doesn't make any difference. I had never been particularly materialistic; but, as I say, an elation was surfacing, sending up preliminary bubbles and, combining with fatigue, washing the evening with a pale, gold wash.

I found a park, a small, enclosed accident of grass, where two roads had failed to meet; I watched a little girl circling on an octagonal, box-like roundabout, screwing herself in and out of my vision. Then I went to a pub. I had plenty of cash; Mr. Purbright had given me an advance.

It was a small, red pub, quiet in the early evening. The landlord moved like a priest; his hands fluttered over the little brass measures; he seemed to tut and keen to himself as he made me a scotch and ginger. Then he gave it to me and withdrew backwards to the back of the bar, where he began to polish something, his hands crawling with the rhythms of humility.

He said, "Are you a visitor to London, Sir? Don't seem to recognise the face," as if he knew all Londoners by sight, and I said, "Yes. Yes, I am."

"Ah," he said. "I see." He obviously felt better; his deficiency of recognition had been explained. Then, "Quiet, now," he said, as if reassuring me, "but it gets busier, later."

"Oh," I said. "I see. That's good."

He walked the length of the bar, performing small, loving

rearrangements of ashtrays; he lifted and examined a drip-mat as if it were a tapestry. The evening sunlight peeled itself from the high windows; dust flickered, tranquil in the air. I said, "I've just inherited over half a million pounds," feeling my throat working in unfamiliar directions.

"Have you, Sir," the landlord said. "I see. Half a million. Half a million."

I said, "Yes. That's right."

"Oh," he said. "Well. Well done, Sir. Very well done."

A few minutes later I had another drink. I offered the landlord one, but he said it was a little early for him; then three suited men came in, and he went off to serve them. It seemed an odd sort of celebration.

I went to bed, about three hours later, in a pleasant hotel room. I wasn't drunk; I hadn't hired a call-girl or two; I hadn't bought champagne all round or been followed from club to club by a crowd of hangers-on. After all, hangers-on were well known to me; my best friend had turned out to be one, in a spectacular kind of way; and Jenny was more competent than any prostitute imaginable. Even then, with the whole lot laid bare, I knew that I wasn't finished with her.

I moved through Trafalgar Square, sending the pigeons into small, messy eddies, wading through the flocks of tourists. I was going to the National Gallery. I should have been going home – Exeter, or Birmingham; but I was enjoying the limbo, the entire anonymity; I seemed to want to prolong it.

I'd never looked at paintings; that's why I was doing it now; I wanted another day out of my life. There were sallow men with forked beards and solid haloes, lamenting over Christ; there was a Madonna, ugly, with a long straight nose, enthroned in a sort of tomb; there was the last judgment, where the whole of the air had become one sedate church, God trapezing from a crossbar, while the damned scuttled below, like suckling piglets, naked and enthusiastic.

I said, to a man in a uniform, "Do you have pictures of ghosts, at all?" and, to his credit, he answered me seriously enough: "Try the Bosch exhibition," he said. White, ascetic nudes coiled inside globular flowers. It seemed to be sex that they were at, but the membranes of canvas held them a long way away. I couldn't see anything like Mrs. Jeffry.

An odd interlude, it was, in London; another brief haunting; myself as ghost. I went home, on the Wednesday; back to Exeter, I mean; a long, flat, sideways drive.

16

Sally's face was a flexible structure strung hard onto a clear framework. Her nose and forehead were a capital T; the hair hung in a single, pointed wave, scratching gently on the cheekbones.

Anger didn't make furrows, in her case; instead, the face stretched, the skin flattened out; the bones showed, white and taut. She was angry for three days; the air in the flat grew slowly opaque with it, with the effort of not saying anything, even though, outside, the growing summer was gouging the countryside.

I couldn't understand it. I suppose that I simply wasn't used to it; used to being regarded, to being missed, to having things expected of me. She said, when I first got back, "You could have let me know, you know," but I had to re-tell the story to myself to make sense of her chagrin. She had phoned me; I had crept off to my mistress; I had disappeared in London. If life had been a soap-opera, then I began to see that Sally would claim the right to a scene of jealousy. I tried to make amends.

We went to Dartmoor, on the Sunday; I remember the tor, close and solid, reduced by the piercing West-Country light. We sat at its foot, glancing up it; it looked like a model, an elegant reach of tidy stone.

"I think I'll climb it," Sally said. "In a bit." She was eating a sandwich; I had made a picnic. She had thawed out, a little; but there was still an air of glum fun.

I said, "It's bigger than it looks." The air was so clear that the summit looked touchable; I didn't want her to strain herself. Notwithstanding my strange behaviour, I loved her, after all.

I opened a can of beer and thought, as I often did, about O'Cleary, passing me a bottle as I looked across the dizzy emptiness of Detford Ridge. Sally said, "How much?" and I said, "Half a million," and she said, "Oh. Good grief." I was lying down, staring straight up into the solid blue sky. Sally was sitting. After a few minutes, she said again, "Good grief," and then she stood, and said, "Are you coming?"

I watched her go. She was bound to be good at climbing – not merely because of her slightness, but because of the lithe balance which seemed to inform her thoughts as well as her deeds. The tor was an abrupt monolith; there were no foothills; she scuttled up the first thirty feet like a spider. The stone picked at her hands and fastened her feet, jutting and folding for her, springing her on and up. There was no point at all in my trying to follow.

After thirty feet, she rested, and then she was off again, combing over the thing as if it were a piece of apparatus. She stood out very clearly, in a red tee-shirt, a red stamp shrinking purposefully on the stone.

I lay back, and, after a time, a swallow took the sun, winging its way exactly between us, eclipsing it in a fleeting pod. I sat up again, and watched the bird as it fielded itself about the air in voluptuous arches. Over and over again it found the one line between the sun and me, slicing darkness into the June afternoon, and I felt myself shiver with each hard blink.

For a long time, it was just the bird and me. It filled the landscape with its black punctuation and my eyes grew weary with its tricks. I suppose that I thought of the empty air; I suppose that I thought of the swallow trudging through the detritus of cramped souls; I tried to see the open sky slurred with struggling spirits, bartering and arguing and grasping at the sun. It was the ghost business; I still couldn't make sense of it.

Mrs. Jeffry said, "There's another one, gone. I told you." Her voice was so close to my ear that the sound was a mouth in itself, a tiny hole in the invisible air, a tiny little pit. I looked around, of course, but I could see nothing, except some children nearby; the Moor was never empty on a hot summer Sunday. I said, "What? What did you tell me?" but the voice was absent, and I knew by then that if she had spoken, it would have been merely to repeat herself: "I told you . . ." I looked up, then, but the swallow had disappeared; the sun blazed, uninterrupted. The tor stood, clean and tidy: Sally had gone.

The old, resigned panic began to lumber up inside me; the old, tired anger began. "There's another one," and I had hoped, for so long, that Mrs. Jeffry had finished with me. "There's another one, gone"; the words caught in my lungs; a stitch hooked itself into my chest as I looked at the small, vacant hill. In some conclusive way, I felt the old woman still there; it seemed to me that she was the only one who stayed, replacing the other women, one by one.

I sat there, on the grass, for quite a long time, looking at the tor, sun plastered all over it. The swallow didn't return, but a tennis-ball bounced across my feet, and a little girl ran across me, after it. I watched her carefully; she seemed to have slight, pinched eyes; she seemed to grimace with bitter lips; for all I knew, she was the old woman, keeping an eye out. The ball puttered right up to the hill, bouncing against it; the child fell on it, and brought it back, giving me a wide berth, this time. I tried smiling, but she looked ahead, pursuing her friends; so I walked to the foot of the tor, and walked carefully round it, until I heard Sally shouting, "Look! Tom! Here!" Her voice hung in the air like a small diamond.

She had climbed around to the other side; that was all. She had gone up, naturally enough, in a spiral; she was waving at me; then, because she could see that I was upset, she was trapezing her way down. She said, "What on earth – ?" and I realised the state of mind I lived in, that death had become the only possible parting. I was frightened of myself, for a moment; I could see the obsession stretching into the future: a child lost in a shop, a wife ten minutes late: dead already, in my mind; the mourning surging away like the sea, for a host of no reasons at all.

The little girl looked hard at me, as we went past to the car. She was like Mrs. Jeffry, all right; especially the child Mrs. Jeffry, the one in the dream, in the photograph that O'Cleary had hidden from me. It was a seventy-year-old face, certainly, strapped into a fragile body; but it had stopped mattering, again. "There goes another one," indeed; but she had been behind a hill, the sharp, June landscape organised beneath her; behind a hill, not dead at all. I hoped then, as I have thought so many times, that it was, in fact, Mrs. Jeffry who was dead, resting, sublime and comfortable, in my mind.

On the way home, Sally said, "Well. You could buy a new car, now. I suppose."

I said, "Yes. I suppose I could." I hadn't thought about the money, in those terms; until then, it had been the slice of an argument. I said, "Yes. I suppose I could buy quite a few things really," and Sally said, "Oh, yes. I suppose you could. With half a million," and we started to laugh. It was a bright giggle, from Sally; she said, "Yes. Well. What do you want to get?"

I thought for a while, and I said, "I think I need a new jacket," and we were laughing a lot, careering through the grey slate of Moretonhampstead. "Oh," said Sally. "I don't know, though. A new jacket? You'll have to keep it cheap," and I said I wouldn't mind a cabin cruiser, and a new house, and some cars. Sally said, "Fine. It's your money. But you want to watch those jackets. You can get carried away," and I remembered Aunt Joyce, laughing at me in the billiard room, after Mrs. Jeffry's death. I thought, too, of Jenny, laying beside me in the crematorium car-park, the puzzled stares of mourners in a far corner. I didn't laugh very often.

Sally said, "Look. Your father. You must go up, you know. He must wonder what happened. Just disappearing, like that." She was very kind. She didn't say, "I told you," even though she had told me, after all, that Father wasn't guilty of deceiving me; she had sensed that he couldn't be, and she had been right. He simply hadn't wanted me to worry, before it was necessary. He had been going to tell me, of course, before my majority, when the lawyers were required to write to me, anyway; but the law had caught him out. That year, 1968, was the year when the age of majority changed; suddenly, overnight, thousands of eighteen-year-olds, like me, had come of age without even having a birthday. It had passed Father by; he was an old man, and rather sick.

That night, I said, "I'll go up tomorrow. Will you come?" I wanted her to. A few moments before she had spread herself across me, lapping, like a cat; I was the milk. I didn't want to be on my own, up in Birmingham, but Sally said, "No. Too busy. You go." She turned carefully onto her side. "Be sure to come straight back," she added, which was a kind of forgiving, and then she went to sleep. I peered for a time into the darkness, wondering how to say sorry for about six years of mistakes.

I was in Birmingham before lunchtime; I had left in the small hours, and watched the sky admit its colour, misted by the dawn. The house hadn't changed; it was a timeless sort of a suburb, fastened by its doors and its stuck-on garages into the 1930s. I never saw anyone go in or out of the houses; I wouldn't know our neighbours by sight.

I was a long time waiting; I had left without my door-key, and it seemed appropriate, now, to be stood in the tiled porch, like a visitor, or a salesman. The house was as silent as a model; it occurred to me that they might be out; they had no reason to be expecting me.

I rang the bell again, checking my pockets, in case I had a spare key; but I hadn't and, anyway, sounds of movement were slowly generating themselves inside. It seemed like about three minutes; but, eventually, Mrs. Malpass opened the door.

She looked hard at me, as if wondering who I was; it seemed possible that she wouldn't let me in; her eyebrows were deep and black. Then she said, rather rudely, "Oh. It's you. Come on, then." Clearly, she shared Father's disapproval of my behaviour; the sudden, unexplained exit, just when it all seemed to be getting better. I thought of apologising, but then I decided that, after all, it really wasn't any of her business. Her shoulders took me towards the dining-room, and she said, "There's some cold stuff, there. For anyone that wants it. I expect you want that, first."

It was a massive slab of ham, the grain gleaming like a sheet of glass, a gingery rind propping it up. There was that, and a bowl of salad; nothing else; a sort of benevolent negligence. I was hungry, at any rate; I filled a plate, and then Mrs. Malpass came back in, and looked at the small hillock of meat, her neck jerking out her disapproval. "Here," she said, with a curtness that was surprising, even in her; she gave me a glass of white wine. It was warm.

I had come to see Father, but I was happy enough to put off the moment for as long as possible. I assumed that he was in bed; presumably, he was no better. Through the french window, the lawn-mower still stood on the patio where I'd left it; the grass itself was curling, luxuriant, scattered with dock-leaves and tiny, waxy buttercups. Perhaps, if all went well, I would mow it, properly, later on.

I was going to play it by ear. I didn't know whether to go through the whole thing, starting six years back, with the will; or just to make up some story about my disappearance last week, and leave it at that. After all, he was an old man, now, to be worrying about history. There was one thing that I was sure about, though; whatever I said, it was going to be what I judged best for him. For the first time in my life, I thought, I was going to be unselfish. Father had had enough. It was up to me to sort him out.

I said to Mrs. Malpass, as she cleared away my plate, "Is Father in bed?"

She stopped, quite still; I couldn't see her face. She said, "Yes."

I said, "Oh, good. Resting," because her silence needed filling with something; but she didn't reply, so I went up the hard, turning staircase, which had a carpet only at its centre, and found Father in the big bedroom.

He looked rather better, oddly enough. The cheeks seemed

to have more colour than last time I'd seen them, when he'd been drinking his Tio Pepe downstairs on the terrace. His eyes were closed, but the skin seemed more relaxed across the bone. I didn't know whether he was asleep, so I said, "Father," quietly, so as not to wake him if he were.

It would have been difficult, of course, to do that. He had been dead for about twenty-four hours, at that point, as I found out, later, from the housekeeper. He had taken a marked turn for the worse, she said, after my unexpected departure; it was clear where Mrs. Malpass placed the blame. He had gone down fast, she said; and, on the Sunday, just before lunch, he has fixed his eyes on something about a yard from his face, smiled at it, and died. Mrs. Malpass had been just about to carve the ham. I, on the other hand, had been sitting on the Dartmoor grass, listening to an old woman's warning, misunderstanding the compressed hiss bursting quietly against my ear.

17

The grass gave up around the island of dry mud, an oval scar, exactly beneath my eyes; something hard to fall on. I tried to press my body sideways, so that, when I fell, it would be onto grass; but she whined at me, the voice rising, a sarcastic siren: "I've never known a scareder boy. Never, never, never!"

I'd got up there on the sheer force of her spite; the fear of going up had been less than the shame of coming down. The tree was in a small, public park; a small, dark crowd of teenagers had gathered, smoking and spitting and laughing at my plight.

Why did she want me to climb a tree? What did it matter to her? She said, I suppose, that it was something an eight-year-old should do; so I was forked rigid across a branch, a small twig shooting painfully into my thigh; and I was about twenty feet up.

It seemed to me that I would be there for ever. The police would have to come, or the fire-brigade, with their ladders; they did it for cats. I could see no way to reverse my impossible ascent; but then she reached out, and shook the branch, which started very low on the trunk. She shook it, so that it waved, slowly; I slid over hard twigs, slowly; I fell, slowly, onto my head. I remember her smile, as I went down. Hours later, I woke up in bed.

It was a Birmingham park; the bed was in Father's house – my house, as it was then. Father was sitting on the edge of the bedspread, when I came round; I said, "Mrs. Jeffry made me fall out of the tree. She shook it. It wasn't my fault."

He sat very still, except for a hand, which passed over his

forehead. "Yes," he said. "Don't worry, Tom. I see." At that time, when I was eight years old, I didn't think that he could possibly see: he seemed to tolerate her unquestioningly; I couldn't see why. Ten years later, the positions were reversed; I sat, like a stowaway, perched on the edge of the bed; now, it was I who didn't understand, after all. Mrs. Malpass came in, and adjusted the bed, as if making it comfortable for an invalid; she plumped the pillow, as if to raise his head, though she was careful not to touch him. Then she was gone, and the day switched to afternoon, the sun cavorting across the window; some flowers appeared, in a vase; the light went out. At one time, I was in bed myself; Father wasn't with me, of course; it was a different bed. A doctor was there, shrinking like a stick man, saying, "Shock," twitching like a puppet. Life geared itself into a series of clicks; flowers came and went, collapsing occasionally into surprising rot, and Mrs. Malpass, speaking an odd, abbreviated language, jerked and stretched about the place like a manic dancer.

Sally came, at one point, and stood straight up, like a mast. The others were growing tiny, laughing on the bed, clustering on the pillows, like pets; I couldn't make sense of any of them. I don't think Jenny came, or O'Cleary; Richard was there, a few times; Clem brought me some fruit, a peach, which dropped into decay, slicing itself unctuously from the stone. I just lay there, for about two weeks, it appears. Then Sally came, and I got up, and the sun started moving about in its usual careful curve and the windows stopped being capricious. A quick breakdown it was, this time; it seemed a shame that Doctor Lister had missed it.

After two weeks, Sally said, "Tom. You're hopeless. We've got to talk about it. If we're going to get married."

We were in the empty garden of the Birmingham house; it was my first day out of bed, and I was sitting at the garden table, where Father had sat, three weeks before. I said, "Talk? Talk about what?"

"About you being hopeless," she said. She wasn't joking; she was sitting on a small, ornamental wall, her bottom resting in a little nest of aubrietia. "I mean," she said. "You still act as if you were twelve. I bet you haven't changed at all. Nervous breakdowns every five minutes. It's a bit wet."

I began to say that two breakdowns in six years wasn't exactly one every five minutes, but I stopped. She was right, after all; I realised that I did see the world still more or less as I had when I was twelve; nobody seemed to have bothered much to educate me, except in the school sense – and that sort of education is designed to keep you young, after all. "Yes," I said, after a while. "Perhaps you're right."

Sally said, "Of course." She managed to say it with no edge of criticism, or arrogance; I was just something to sort out; it wasn't my fault. She added, "You haven't made a decision for years. You're not a kid, any more. Time for a change." She sat down beside me, picking up my glass of scotch, and finishing it. "That bitch Jenny hasn't helped," she said.

I said, "What? You haven't . . . ?" and Sally replied, "Oh, yes. 'Course I have. At the funeral."

I hadn't been; I'd been in bed. As my fiancée, Sally had gone, instead. Obviously, she had met Jenny. I hadn't really thought about it.

"Yes," she said. "Oh, yes. I can quite see the point, there. My word, yes."

I said, "What do you mean? 'The point'?"

"The point," she said, "of your incestuous obsession."

I said, "It isn't incest. Not with a cousin . . ." but she interrupted me. "No," she said. "No. I know. It was a joke." We sat in silence for quite a long while. A blackbird found one of the apple trees, scaling up a ladder of song; I noticed that a small detachment of snails was occupying a corner, where two walls joined. I watched them, static in their little, spiral assurance, spread straight and dogged on the crazy paving.

Sally said, "She's quite a girl. Extraordinary." She spoke musingly, as if to herself. "Two dimensions. I tried to get round her. See her from behind. It's like trying to see round the back of a mirror."

I said, "I hate her. Actually," because it was true, and it seemed that it might be the right thing to say.

She said, "Oh, yes. I should think you do. Parts of her, at any rate. Parts. Then again, there must be some parts you don't mind at all."

"Look," I said. "I didn't know I was going to meet you. Did I? Be fair. You can't blame me for things that happened before."

"No," she said. "That's true. I can't. But I can blame you for anything that happens from now on, can't I? That must be part of the bargain."

She looked hard at me. I said, "Nothing will happen. We're going to get married. Jenny's finished. Honestly."

Sally said, levelly, "You'll have to stop doing this, you know. I don't think anybody's ever told you what's what. How to behave. You don't just tell lies for your own convenience. Kids do that. 'Jenny's finished.' Come off it."

"Yes," I said. "Well. It's difficult." I told her, then, about what had happened in the lodge; about driving down there, finding them in bed, discovering that they both despised me, that they had despised me for years. "I hate her," I said again. "And him. I'd thought he was a friend." I always seemed to speak like that; life turned flat when it went into words; a series of disjointed statements.

"Can you promise me," Sally said presently, slowly, "that if we get married, you won't go to her again? Ever again?"

I looked at the snails, grim and static; I looked at the mower; I searched the web of the apple tree for the blackbird that was still bursting about in there, singing at its blossom. I was on the beach, and Jenny was stretching, arching her back to let the sun in, pouring herself over the sand. "Who's going to oil me?" she was saying. "I need oiling. Tom. Come here." I watched O'Cleary: he was called Tom, too, but he didn't move. "It's you she's meaning," he said, all grinning; and she held out the tube, and said, "Good boy. Back and legs. Plenty."

My hands shook, as I did it; I'd been fourteen; I hadn't even slept with her, then. I squeezed it onto my palm, and began to rub her, from the neck, across to the shoulders; she felt hot. It was a one-piece swimsuit, but the back was cut low; I worked into the aperture, contouring my fingers over the shoulder-blades; she was lying on her stomach, reading a magazine. "Legs," she said. "Top of legs." O'Cleary watched with amusement; he winked at me; I smiled, uncertainly; it was a bit like learning to swim. She moved her feet slightly apart, so that my hands could round her thighs; I carved and wheedled at them, terrified, pocketing my fingers between them. "Don't miss any," she said. "I'll be cross if I burn," and O'Cleary laughed out loud, and I folded myself into not missing any, until Jenny said, "Enough." I lay down on my own stomach, then; O'Cleary went for a swim. After a while, Jenny turned over, and said, "He's like a big kid." She sat up, watching him swimming; he was a strong swimmer; in no time at all, he was out past the pier.

I said, "O'Cleary? A kid? What do you mean?"

"Oh," she said. "I don't know. A big show-off." She chuckled, and I laughed, too, because I liked laughing with Jenny. I said, "Remember when he turned up? When she snuffed it? I couldn't believe my eyes."

"Mmm," she said. "Yes. Christ. I thought it was a ghost." She laughed again. "My God," she said. "So did you!" He had disappeared; he used to swim right round the bay, delivering himself sveltely onto some other beach. The water was as much his element as the air; he bashed them both about, shaping them into his shape, curling himself in and out. I said, "Do you like him?" It was him I was interested in; I wanted to see whether she shared my fixation; it hadn't occurred to me to be jealous.

"He's all right," she said. She was sixteen, then, and, presumably, sharing his bed every night; but she said, "He's all right," and, "He's like a big kid," and she picked up the sun-tan oil again.

She squeezed a bulb of it onto two finger-tips, and she glanced at me, her grin lazy and open. "Front, now," she said. "Which, of course, I can manage on my own. Without any help from little boys," and she managed it, in hypnotic circles dipping from the bones of her neck. Sally said, "Come on. Answer. It's important."

She was still on the garden wall. The snails were still there; the blackbird had bustled off. "Go on," she said. "I'm saying, promise you won't go to her again."

I watched her carefully, for a time. I was feeling much better. The breakdown had been as much about Mrs. Jeffry as it had been about Father's death; that is, his death seemed yet another piece of evidence, since the old woman had warned me of it, announcing it in my ear on Dartmoor at the exact time of its happening. But she hadn't spoken again; and in some strange way, I was beginning to find her concern reassuring. Father's death had been a surprise, and of course I felt guilty about it; but we hadn't actually been friends for years.

After a fortnight of hallucinations, my head felt oddly clear; empty, earthy, like a garden after rain. So I looked at Sally, and, not because I thought it was the right thing to say; nor because I thought it would please her; but actually because it was the truth, I said: "No." I was seeing the fingers, glistening in the hollow of the neck. "No," I said. "I'm sorry. It's not how I want it. But I can't promise."

It was a sigh that came from her; a long, slow release. "Thank God for that," she said, after the sigh. "Perhaps we're finally getting somewhere," and after lunch we were off to the West Country to make plans for the wedding.

18

It was an indifferent day. The big house was at its best in sunshine, when the shadows gave it shape; or in frost or snow, which gave it a flaky, Dickensian authority; but in summer rain, it simply looked what it was: massive, impractical, ugly. I was walking quickly up between the rowans, sheltering from one to the next, looking at the place, wondering why, after seven years of ownership, I hadn't got round to selling it.

Sally was in the kitchen. "Hot in the summer," she said. "Cold in the winter. That's the way I like it. You know where you are."

I said, "It's not the first bad summer I've spent here." It was 1975; we'd been married seven years; but I was thinking of the year of Mrs. Jeffry's death, when the rowans had curled in the wind.

Sally said, "There's a man in the lounge. Council," so I went in to see him. Not infrequently, they came up for donations, for worthy causes. As Sally used to say, I was half a millionaire.

I said to him, "I'm so sorry to keep you."

He stood up. "Mr. Fellows," he said. "My name's Bright. Town Council. Please forgive intrusion."

I gave him a drink. He said, "On duty!" and knocked it back anyway, screwing his immensely tall frame back into three-quarters of the settee.

"Well," he said; a young man; about my age, with a middle-aged suit. "Get to the point. Point is, Mr. Fellows. Pier. The pier."

The old pier was still clinging onto the land – gripping the cliff, as it were, with one or two fingers. I looked at it most days, now that we lived there; I often wondered when they were going to do something about it; an increasing area of the beach was becoming closed to the public, for safety reasons.

Mr. Bright spoke like a memo. He said, "Problem is. Council really does feel, now; pier must go. Half the beach unusable, so on. Safety hazard, so on. Eyesore, sort of thing."

Sally came in, with some tea; Bright had some, to go with his whisky. He said, "You," as he took it.

"I see," I said. "Well. It seems a shame. But I've no doubt you're right. How can I help? Is there some problem with funding? Or is it access?"

"No problem, funding," said young Mr. Bright, trying so hard to be older, to be pressed for time, to be important. "Of course, access, problem. Pier stands against your land."

I said, "But of course, you can have access. Any time you like. How do you go about it? Do you just knock it into the sea? Or do you try to haul it back onto the land?"

Mr. Bright didn't know. He thought that they would dismantle it superficially and then pull away the supports, picking up the pieces from the sea after it had fallen. I said, "Well. It seems a shame. But I suppose there's nothing else for it."

Mr. Bright began to uncoil his legs. "No," he said. "That's point. So. Bring you over some documents to sign. Council will arrange all works, present you with account."

I said, "Hang on. What? Account? What do you mean?"

Mr. Bright's expression never altered. He peered at his cup of tea, as if slightly but agreeably puzzled by it. "Well," he said. "To be fair, Mr. Fellows. Hardly expect Council foot the bill. Very patient, in the circumstances. Your pier, after all."

Purbright confirmed it, on the telephone. "I did send you copies of these papers," he said, defensively. "She owned a fair bit of property around the town. Including the old pier." I remembered her taking me on there, helping me with the slot-machines: her slot-machines. I said to Sally, "She was extraordinary."

"Are you going to let them?" she asked me. "Pull it down?"

I said, "I don't suppose I can stop them. I'm probably breaking the law by having it there anyway. I don't know."

Sally said, "You need someone to look after all this, you know. I keep telling you. I mean, owning things you don't even know you own. It's ridiculous."

I suppose that it was. I'd looked through the papers, originally; there were many of them, and of course the language was far from clear. Doubtless, the pier was referred to as something else entirely. At any rate, I'd had no idea that it was mine and, since its existence impinged upon nobody else, except the Town Council, nobody else had pointed it out.

"Well," Sally said. "I'll be glad to see it go. Every time I look at it, I think of that little bitch leading you on." I said, "Come on . . ." but she continued, "No. I mean it. You could quite easily have dropped through that bloody hole and drowned yourself. And she knew it. Cow."

The rain stopped. I said, "Come on. Let's go and have a look at it," and we left the kitchen, cutting through the rowan avenue, up to the cliff. The notices about danger were well weathered, by now; nobody ever went up there. It was my land, though there was a public footpath across it which no-one ever used. Sally said, "It's a funny place. For a pier. I mean, they usually go from the sea-front, don't they? I mean, the promenade."

I hadn't thought of it. I said, "Yes. I suppose this footpath was used a lot more." She was right, though: the pier led from the top of a hill – "the cliff", as we used to call it – which meant that it was particularly high, over the water; austere as a suspension bridge. We stood and watched it, for a time, as the wind took itself up from the water and threw our voices into our throats, jamming our ears, muffling our heads, carving us out on the tiny promontory. The pier lurched, yanking at the hill, so that with each crack or swing of its length it seemed to move the ground itself, pulling the very hill forward into the water. Sally yelled something against my head, but I heard nothing, so she rammed her mouth into my ear, and I heard: "I'll give you a kiss if you walk it for me . . ."

She was right, in the sense that it would have been no more dangerous, then, than it had been twelve or thirteen years ago; but I was growing tired of jokes about Jenny, and set off back to the house alone. After seven years of marriage, I still saw my cousin, regularly, though not often; and Sally knew all about it.

I'd tried lying, for the first few months, but Sally wouldn't have it. Fooling myself was easy enough; driving off to London, where Jenny now lived, telling myself that it was the last time; but Sally was less easy to convince. One night, when I'd got back late, she'd said to me, "It's all got to stop, you know," and I'd thought she'd meant my meetings with Jenny; but she hadn't. "What I won't have," she said, sitting up in bed, in the house we still called "Mrs. Jeffry's house," "is the lying."

I was wretched; ashamed, and embarrassed by discovery. I said, "But everybody lies. They do. Aunt Joyce . . ." I was remembering my beautiful, sad auntie, sitting beside me, above the lake; I was remembering the notion of the gel of lies, the membranes of lies, thick in the air; a new discovery, then, but one that had been confirmed, since then, every day, by almost everyone I knew.

"Oh, I know that," she said – even though, of all the people I've ever met, I think she is the one who does, in fact, tell the truth, always. "I know that, Tom. It's not the point. There's lies, and there's lies. You've got it out of hand. All those years fibbing to your father've done it. You don't lie to people like that. People like me. Not to people who are supposed to matter."

I said, "I told you, before we were married. You asked me, and I told you. I said I couldn't promise to keep away from her. I told you."

"Yes," she said. "Yes, you did. That's why it's pointless

lying about it now. I mean. 'Been to a meeting.' What do you think I am?"

I had, in fact, been sitting on the floor in a corner of Jenny's flat; she had been laughing at me. "So," she'd been saying. "Married life isn't quite satisfactory, after all. Not quite entirely satisfying. Poor Tom. But, of course, I don't sleep with married men . . ." but she had, of course; she had led me to her bedroom, and humiliated me, and never stopped laughing for a moment. Now, Sally said, "We'll work something out about this. In the morning," and she put the light out, and I undressed in the dark.

Seven years later, we sat in the kitchen and Sally repeated, "Well. I'm glad it's coming down. It's a wonder no-one's been killed," and we both thought of Jenny, who hadn't been sorted out at all, who still hung about, whose breath still worked like silk on the back of my mind. O'Cleary had disappeared, when he'd realised that he was getting nothing; the lodge had simply emptied itself of him, though all the ornaments were still there. He'd been allowed it by Father as a sort of concession to fair play; I suppose that he wasn't going to ask favours of me. He disappeared – back to Ireland, I supposed; and we moved in to the big house, saying how awful it was, and how we were going to sell it and live somewhere decent, in the country, where I could paint pictures. I'd taken to painting pictures, as a hobby; I didn't have to work for a living, though I kept an office, in the town, to manage the estate. There were four houses, all tenanted, and various part-shares of businesses; I owned some of a fish and chip shop and half of the Bermuda Guest House. And, as it turned out, the pier.

After seven years, we still hadn't got round to moving; we still haven't. I suppose that, all along, I have wanted the rowan avenue, the berries simply there one August morning, the wind working ineffectually amongst the branches; so I made one of the bedrooms into a sort of studio, and painted pictures in it from time to time. They were not much good.

* * *

Mr. Bright wrote me a letter, telling me how many thousands of pounds it was going to cost to pull the pier down. I showed it to Joyce; she came often to see us; she had become fond of Sally. It was a warm August afternoon, in 1975. A year later there was a drought; the days blistered into one; but in 1975 a warm afternoon was an event. So we sat in the back garden, drinking tea or, in my case, wine. Jenny would have drunk wine; though not too much.

"What was she doing," I asked, "owning a pier?"

Joyce sighed. She grew prettier, as she grew older; the melancholy seemed more becoming. "As far as I know," she said, "she married into it. I think what happened was, that she holidayed here, once or twice, as a small child. Over from Ireland. They weren't all that well off. I don't know. But then she married Mr. Jeffry, who was. And she made him buy this place. It meant a lot to her. And old Jeffry, he speculated around and about, just for the interest. He had plenty. So I suppose he just bought it.

"Anyway," she added. "That's what I think happened. Roger got that from your father. Over the years."

Sally said, "And. Whatsisname. O'Cleary happened, presumably, before Mr. Jeffry."

I wondered what Joyce thought about that. O'Cleary had slept with her daughter for years, when her daughter had been no more than a girl, a schoolgirl, probably, who also slept with me, because I was going to be rich. Who, in fact, still slept with me, because I was rich. It seemed impossible that we could be together, exactly in a triangle, drinking tea on a flat lawn in the moulded shade of a crab-apple tree. So comfortable, we must have looked to any passer-by who glanced in over the hedge; so static, Sally and Joyce smiling at each other in a knowing way they'd developed.

Sally started clearing away; I think that the plates clattered a little sharply on the edge of the afternoon; her mind had turned to Jenny, too, and she was irritable. They went inside together; I don't know what intimacies they shared; I don't know how much they knew. I watched my glass of wine for a time, and wondered what to do with it, and then I drank it and filled it and drank it again. What troubled me was that the marriage was a happy one; I didn't understand how it could be; I didn't see how Sally could accept it, how she could be irritated by it, banging cups onto a tray, and yet smile and clean the house and look carefully after me as I went about. Neither could I see how I could watch for her, and wait at night, unble to concentrate on my book, for her to come upstairs; I didn't see how I could love her, and still need the other thing, the trip to London for what Sally sometimes called my "family reunions". In a certain mood, she laughed about them; and that, of course, was the worst mood of all.

I had a word with Mrs. Jeffry about it. I chatted to her often, at that time; I discussed problems with her. The back lawn was a favourite spot for it; so was the rowan avenue, because you could see anybody coming, and stop nattering to yourself. Once or twice I had tried it in the office, asking her in a wheedling sort of way what I should do about the Yeos, who managed the Bermuda Guest House fairly awfully, or about the big house itself; but Mrs. Golley, who was my secretary, caught me at it, so I stopped. They were helpful chats; my voice passed into a new level, the words embroidered on the air. She never answered, of course; I hadn't heard a thing from her since that Sunday on Dartmoor when she'd told me that my father was dead and I hadn't understood. Nevertheless, I spoke to her, quite freely; Sally had got used to it.

"I don't know if you're in favour, or not," I said. I was moaning; it was a complaint. "You used to warn me off her. Then you said the opposite . . ." but I knew it was no use trying to make sense of her. If she had any motive at all, it was simple entertainment; the turns in the plot were there just for their own sake. Nevertheless, "What the hell am I going to do?" I asked, squinting just above the willow at the opaque, blue sky, listening to the silence. I suppose that it was like praying.

They stopped talking as I went in, and Joyce said she had to go, and kissed me; there was no hostility. Sally smiled, and pottered off, and there I sat, splayed at the centre of Mrs.

Jeffry's house and money and manipulations. After a time, and as usual, I began to think about Jenny.

"I don't know," she said, very slowly. "I'm awfully tired, Tom. I've been up late, a lot. I don't think I can be bothered with you. Not tonight . . ."

"But you . . . It's arranged," I said pathetically. "You said . . ."

She stood up. "Whatever I said," she said, "I'm entitled to change my mind." She paused. "Aren't I?" she added.

I was standing. It was Jenny's flat, and I sat down when I was told. She had been seated, on one of the sofas; she was wearing a long, shapeless housecoat; when she stood, it parted slightly; the leg was perfectly turned. I was trembling, very slightly, at the thought of what might or might not be about to happen.

It was an expensive flat. She did well, did Jenny – out of people like me. Perhaps O'Cleary had taught her; or perhaps it came naturally, the settees and the jewellery and the rent squeezed deftly from the ecstasy of others. She let the housecoat fall; her underwear was expensive, too. Some sort of black top, and then the legs, wrenched into the stockings, the feet pumped into the high heels. It is, I realise, the description of a prostitute.

She stood, looking at me, and then she stepped over the housecoat, walking towards me, smelling of violets. She stood very close, then, her face inches from mine, but I knew that I mustn't touch her. She said, "Is it very bad? Mmm? Have you got it very badly indeed?" and I said, immediately, "Oh, yes. It's very bad indeed. If I could just . . .", but she had turned away and was walking towards the bedroom door. "Pick that up," she murmured, as she stepped on the negligee, so I did, following her. "Stay out," she said, quietly. "I'm getting changed. You can take me to dinner," and I sat on her sofa, then, waiting, hearing her moving, and telephoning, and laughing, for three-quarters of an hour.

Finally, she stood before me, in a white dress that made her look more naked than she had before. "Like?" she said, and I said, "Oh, yes. Yes . . ." and she said, quickly, "Where's Sally?"

"Oh," I said. "At home. I . . ."

"I didn't know," Jenny said, very seriously. "Tights," she went on, looking down, "or stockings." My throat was dry, as she knew. "Tights," she said. "Or stockings." I imagined men queueing to pay her just to say the words. "Anyway," she said, after a while, "I decided. Stockings. Actually."

"Not," she added casually, filling a leather handbag with something, "that it will make any difference to you at all. None at all," and she gave me her front door-key and we were in the corridor. "Unless," she murmured, as an afterthought, "you're a very good boy indeed."

19

Doctor Lister looked well: sleek on the tasty stew of nervous breakdowns. I saw him, as I often did, near the sea-front; he said, "Good morning." I don't think that he remembered me as a twelve-year-old patient; he knew me vaguely as someone well-off who bobbed about on various committees. "Hello," I said, politely, but I was looking past him, towards the High Street. It was empty, except for Mrs. Jeffry, who was standing quite still, at the far end. It was the same filthy, old skirt, folded inside the legs; the same, dirty old face, the skin built solid beneath the eyes, the lids horizontal, like flaps.

There wasn't much point in walking towards her; I knew that. Although she didn't speak, any more, these appearances were common enough. I would start towards her, and then I would become distracted, and she would be gone. There might be no-one about; or there might be crowds, drilling themselves into expert little bus-queues; whatever happened, I would lose her, and it would be my own fault. I don't know why she came; I couldn't even tell if she were looking at me; the eyes hung on her face.

Autumn was nosing about the town; it was, after all, the right season for the end of the pier. They'd been at it for several days already, sticking even bigger barriers around the bottom, installing various bits of marine machinery and balancing a crane on the headland. Sally and I had been up on the first day, but it was unspectacular; Mr. Bright told us it would be a week or so before anything dramatic happened. He was up there, in his suit, and a yellow, metal hat.

We stood there, anyway, for an hour or two. There were

about a dozen men, working roughly as a chain, removing the fittings. Someone had put up a painted sign, which read: LIFE JACKETS MUST BE WORN; but we couldn't see any. The entrance barrier had been removed and men swayed in and out, on and off, carrying rusted iron slot-machines and deckchairs with only wisps of canvas; skeleton after skeleton of municipal fun. Bright said, unexpectedly, "Where do you want this stuff?" and I realised that it belonged to me. Sally said, "Oh. Dump it," but I was watching two men carrying the rotted boards of a fortune-teller's booth, another man nursing the dead weight of a PRIZE EVERY TIME, its glass globe intact, a neat but filthy cage for its wire chicken and its heap of promises. "No," I said. "No. Hang on. Let's think."

The finest thing about the pier was the lettering: the thinnest tracery along both sides: WEST PIER – AMUSEMENTS. The letters stretched like lace, a filigree of cast iron. I don't know why they called it the West pier; there was only ever one of them.

At the far end, the toffee-apple hut stood; for some reason, they couldn't seem to shift it. "Doesn't matter," someone said, to Mr. Bright. "It can go down with the rest of it," and Bright asked me if that was all right, and I confirmed that I didn't have any pressing need for a toffee-apple hut, and then we went back to the house. "I hope he tells us," said Sally. "I want to see it. When it goes down."

I told Jenny about it, over dinner. "Some time next week," I said. "About Wednesday."

She laughed. "Shall I come?" she said, looking past me, at a waiter, whom she'd said was attractive.

I said, "Good God. No. What do you mean?"

"It's all right," said Jenny. "Trust me. Remember Toby?" A huge dessert arrived; it looked like a little ocean itself; we started to giggle. "Now," she said. "Now. O'Cleary. That was a man, all right. I would have gone with him, if he'd have had me. Never mind. There we are. There's others." She turned slightly petulant; the champagne popped her eyes; then she giggled, again. "I bet Sally doesn't wear stockings," she said.

"I bet she hasn't got a pair." I was trying to interrupt; I knew where we were going; but she went on. "I bet," she said, "they don't make them short enough."

I didn't laugh, at any rate. I didn't join in the joke, though, I suppose, I would have done, at that time, if forced. It was, after all, only a version of Jenny's self-love; and I concurred in that. I fought it off, though, for the moment; I ducked beneath the humiliation, though I knew that it would come later, that same evening, when she would say, "Well? Would you? Would you?" and, because she was standing over me, the dress unzipped, a shoulder out, white as a bone, I would say, whatever the condition, "Yes. Yes. I would . . . "

Mr. Bright called it, rather unfortunately, "P-Day". If we went up, he said, on the telephone, if we were interested, we should see the stricken superstructure buckle into itself, cower, waver and dive. Or, to be more precise, Mr. Bright said we should be able to see it go under.

It was a brilliant September morning. Colour was blocked in everywhere; the eye almost cringed against the slant of the black sky. From the cliff we could see the whole of the beach, the whole of the little, English bay, the cliffs rigid and dented, like gums. The trippers had gone home but two or three dozen locals had gathered on the sand to see the old pier go. There had been an article in the local paper.

Sally said, "What a day!" The air stood so still around us that our voices seemed to hold it; the end of the pier looked touchable; the horizon of sea looked like something carefully arranged by a painter. There was a festive atmosphere; people on the beach had picnic baskets and cameras; there was a rumour that Local T.V. was on the way. The pier looked more dangerous than ever, without its trivial topping to weight it down. A strange idea, altogether, it occurred to me: a short trip to nowhere, an unfinishable path. You could see the length of its thin lines, now; you could see the kiosk, over fifty yards away, swaying like the cabin of a fishing-boat.

We, alone, watched from the hill, like guests in the royal

box. A reporter climbed up and asked me what I thought. "Is it," he asked, "a small piece of history dying before our eyes?"

I said, "What? It's . . ." and Sally said, "Don't be daft. It's a dangerous old eyesore," and the reporter smiled and went away. The next Friday I was recorded in his paper as having "mourned" the pier's end. "It was," I said, apparently, "a piece of old history." And, of course in a sense, it was. For me.

What happened was that the crane was fastened in turn to each of the great upright wooden trunks which formed the pier's legs. It pulled, and, with a fairly explosive snap, the leg came away and the pier sagged. It was a disappointingly obvious process. After the first snap, the audience managed a tiny roar which hung about twelve feet over their heads in the viscous autumn sunshine. The pier rearranged itself, making a small obeisance, re-shuffling, losing bits which it showered musically into the water. The tide was in.

We began to see that it was going to be a long day. There were a fair few of these pillars and, because the men were working progressively outwards from land to sea, the thing wouldn't fall until they took out the last one or two, at the far end. People began to mooch off; after a while, Sally asked me to take her shopping, and we disappeared, too, after calculating how long it was going to take.

Doctor Lister would have said that it was symbolic. The passing of the pier was the passing of my adolescence, he would have judged, sitting like a paperweight behind his empty desk. A very important moment, he would have said. After all (polishing his clean glasses), a pier is an obvious symbol of male potency, anyway. That is probably why they were built. And (setting straight the tiny angle of his unopened notebook), in my particular circumstances . . .

The sad truth is that I didn't care at all. If Jenny hadn't caught me there, she would have caught me somewhere; and, anyway, I was glad to be caught. I wasn't glad to be glad; but I was glad to be caught. We went back up there in the late afternoon; the brilliance had gone out of the day; the light was beginning to blot itself down into the water; but we could see the last two pillars out there, the pier still aloft like a broken spring between them and the hill.

Mr. Bright was flustered. Various strangers in overcoats were standing in tight, critical groups; breath was filming the air. "What's up?" I said to him, and he spread his hands, slightly, and said, "Oh. It's the county engineer. He says . . . Well. The contractors are making a bit of a muck of it. He says. Apparently. They should work inwards; towards the shore. Safer, so on. Whole lot's going to go at once, instead of a bit at a time. Had to support it, middle."

He pointed, and I saw that some sort of jack had caught the centre, rooting it back down to the sea. "Should have removed all the boards," Mr. Bright added. "Floor. Just left the uprights."

I could see the sense in that, too. There was no need for any of the superstructure, I thought; no-one was ever going to walk down there again. "Still," said Bright, philosophically. "Done now." His face was red – only partly from the fine evening chill which was slicing carefully down from the clear, dark sky. One or two stars were out.

"Oh, well," I said; I wanted him to relax. "Never mind."

"Yes," said Bright. "No. Have to leave it up, though, probably. Getting dark. Finish it tomorrow," and I thought of the pier heeling over in the first mists, finally. It occurred to me that the thing was becoming a bore.

I looked round for Sally, to take her back home; but I couldn't see her. People were packing up, now; the pier itself looked deserted; the men in hats were getting into cars. "Have you seen my wife?" I asked Bright, but he hadn't; the old panic began; slow, reluctant, turning in its cold radius. She wasn't on the little headland; she wasn't on the cliff; as far as I could see, she wasn't on her way home, either.

She was, in fact, on the pier. It was by no means dark; I could see her, suddenly quite clearly, about fifteen yards in, treading the board along the side, moving slowly outwards. Bright came with me; so did several others; I stood at the entrance and shouted at her.

She turned. "There's somebody out there!" she called. She was quite calm – the only one who was. "I saw somebody. Right at the end. It's not safe."

Bright said, "Impossible," and I called, "Sally. Come back. It's not possible!" The pier curled itself unctuously, stretched luxuriously; after a fine day, the wind was getting up. Mr. Bright called, "Mrs. Fellows! Mrs. Fellows! I must ask you – " but Sally yelled, "I saw her! Old woman . . ." and then immediately I understood so I called, "Sally!" She had set off again, and the pier was rolling joyfully, bristling and flexing.

"Sally!" I shouted. "Come here! I'll go, instead."

"Don't be daft!" she called; but at least she stopped walking, and turned towards us. "You can't even swim!" I knew it; I had no intention of walking the pier for a second time; certainly not in the pursuit of a filthy old ghost. I was lying, again; that was why it felt so familiar.

I shouted "Come back! I'll go! I'm safer. I've done it before!"

She stood, holding the rail behind her with both hands, like a gymnast. She was in every way better qualified than I to attempt such a rescue; but I wasn't going to let her. No voice had hissed in my ear; the air hadn't opened in a short jet of spite; but I knew that the old woman was behind this, somewhere.

Bright said, "If I may say so, Mr. Fellows . . . Must get her off. Not safe at all, now . . ."

The darkness was holding off; I could see it, up in the sky, a slate line, the shadow of the world. The little bay clenched itself around us; the water pinched itself into lips as the wind spiralled about. I said, "No-one could have got on there? Surely?" and Bright said, "No. There's been nobody up here . . ." and he was right.

I called, "Come on. Come back! I'll go!" and Sally stood as the pier rode like the sea itself, waving, drawing and breaking like the water below. "Come on!" I shouted. "I know who it is! I'll explain . . .!" and then Sally had turned and was walking, stepping against the tide of the pier, clambering up through the air, back to the land.

Her face was white; the wind had tightened the skin; she said, "All right. Go on. Only you'd better mean it." She was shivering; it had turned very cold. Bright said, "If I . . ." and I said, "It's all right, Mr. Bright. No-one's going on there. Don't worry."

She stopped shaking. There was the slightest of pauses; then she said, "What?"

I said, "Look. Come here. Over here." To Mr. Bright, I said, "Excuse us," and we walked away, Sally saying, "You . . . You said you'd go. There's an old lady on there. She'll never get off, on her own. You said . . .!"

I said, "Look. Listen. I know. I know what I said. But listen. There's no-one there. There's no need . . ."

Sally was very angry. "If you could get on with it," she said. "Only there's someone on that bloody monstrosity and, thanks to Mr. Bright and his merry team of incompetents, she's about to snuff it."

I said, "No. Look. Black coat? Seventy-ish? Just standing there?" She nodded, and I said, "Jeffry. It's Mrs. Jeffry. Isn't it? I've told you I see her. That's her. It's nobody. It's some sort of trick . . ."

There was an immense noise, then; a shattering of glass, a grinding of metal. We looked up; the pier was listing; the tide seemed to be shifting it, working it like a puppeteer. Sally said, "Thomas. You promised. God knows why I came back. I could have had her off there by now."

Bright was coming over; the few remaining men were clearing off, in various ways; the overcoats had long gone. I said, "I've told you . . ." but Sally said, "I've told you about lies . . ."

I said, "It isn't a lie. I'm telling you!"

"No," said Sally. "I mean going on there. You told me you'd go. Now get on there, up to the end. The far end. She's behind that hut thing."

I opened my mouth, but she said, "Look. I don't know about your bloody ghost, but I know this. You see her. You. Not me." She was walking again, back to the pier, which was barricaded again, with a brand-new notice: UNSAFE – ENTRY

ABSOLUTELY PROHIBITED. "You?" she said, over her shoulder. "Or me?"

Later, the irony struck me: she was repeating Jenny's hated request of twelve or more years ago. It didn't occur, at that moment; all I thought of was the walk I was going to have to do, avoiding not a small hole a third of the way down but the constant wrecking and twisting of the thing on the air itself. Sally wasn't being rhetorical; she meant that she would do it, if I wouldn't; but that, of course, was impossible, so I folded myself through the barrier, for the second time in my life, and, choosing a path exactly on the edge, I began to trapeze my way along.

It still wasn't dark; that would come suddenly, I knew, down like a stopper on the bay. I could see no old woman, when I looked up; but I didn't look up very often. There was a decent length of wooden board, all along the edge; but I had to watch it, as it was constantly, restlessly finding new ways to lie, so that my feet were surprised and confused, and each step was a changing experiment. It was almost a game, to predict where the pier would put itself, how it would shrug away its support. If I dropped down, I'd be dead; I knew that – perhaps better than Sally did. The water was quite turbulent, in autumn high tides; the currents countered each other; and, anyway, it would be pretty cold. So I watched the floor, and held the rail, treating both with a sort of deference, allowing them to shake and run me as they wished.

It was simply like that, for the length of the pier. I looked neither forward nor back; I just worked my way along to the end until finally I was standing landward of the kiosk, wondering what I was going to find, if anything, on the other side. I remember noticing that the wind and salt had stripped off all the paint, revealing parts of an earlier, enamel notice on the side of the hut. Where it had said "TOFFEE-APPLES", it had once, apparently, said, "ICE". I wondered what it meant, for a few seconds; then I began to move around the hut, and there, between the shutters and the sea, was Mrs. Jeffry, who smiled warmly at me, and said, "Oh. You'll do," at the moment that the pier collapsed and, in complete silence, I was sluiced feet-first through the web of wood and into the sea, slicing rigidly down to the centre of the black water, wondering why I could hear nothing at all.

20

The sun worked exquisitely behind the crab-apple tree, lacing the branches, sewing the leaves together, dropping a perfect shadow onto the lawn. It was the finest summer I could ever remember behind the big house. I could see each apple separately; bright purple, they were; not the usual faint yellow; highly coloured, though undersized. I was at a white table, spread with cakes and sponges: a childish feast; it seemed to please me.

The brothers were playing, over near the willow, in front of the hedge; I could hear Clem shouting and laughing. I sat alone, and wondered whether I could try a cake. They were lined up in sumptuous little avenues, sugar crumbling onto the table-cloth. There was a jug of thick, home-squeezed lemonade.

"That's the stuff," said Mrs. Jeffry, smiling. She had come out of the back door, with a tray of sandwiches, white, triangular. The air soothed us both; the sun lifted smiles from us; Mrs. Jeffry said, "There. That's the stuff." She was talking about the lemonade. "Not like you buy in the shops."

After a while, I said, "May I have some? Or should I wait? For the others?"

She smiled again – looking like O'Cleary. "Wait?" she said. "Oh, I don't think so. No, Tom. Why wait? You enjoy yourself."

I was very hungry. Mrs. Jeffry disappeared into the kitchen; I could hear laughter; there were others in there. It seemed odd, to be feasting alone; surely the brothers should come, or Jenny?

Father didn't seem to think that it mattered. He wandered onto the lawn, laughing at something; Mother was with him, smiling shyly in my direction; they came over, and sat with me. Mother said, gently, "It's nice to have you here, Tom," and I noticed that she was scratching a finger, a middle finger, as though she'd been bitten by a summer insect. I said, "It's warm," because it was, and because I wanted to be polite, and Father said, "Yes. Humid. Midges," and Mother carried on rubbing.

I said, "Where's Jenny?" and Mrs. Jeffry laughed, and said, "Oh. She'll join us soon enough. Won't I do, instead?" and Father laughed and Mother smiled shyly across the table. I noticed that, as she rubbed it, the skin peeled itself into little shavings, dropping in curls onto her plate. The sun held itself very still, stretching carefully around the shape of each of us; the light piled up against the garden wall and shivered inside the hedge, driving itself in wedges at the house itself. Mother had now rubbed all of the skin away, exposing the bone, white, jointed, polished like pearl. She held it up, briefly, as if examining her nail-varnish; the bone and little tendons stood up like a tiny sailing-ship.

It was very hot indeed; Mrs. Jeffry poured me some more lemonade; I noticed that the nose had gone from her face. In the kitchen, I heard O'Cleary laugh; I heard Jenny shout, "Tom!"; I wanted to join them; they were my friends. I tried to stand, but Mother said, "Tom! Do finish first," and Mrs. Jeffry said, "Manners!" and they smiled at each other and at Father. "After all," said Mrs. Jeffry, "I'm as good as Jenny, any day, aren't I?" and, indeed, it was Jenny's face that she had, then, the eyes fastening round the corners of the cheeks. Mother and Father laughed, and I laughed, too, as if at some trick.

Every line of me sweltered and I said, "Is it possible to have some ice? With the lemonade?" but I had said the wrong thing. Mother and Father looked at each other and then at the old woman, who breathed in deeply, her face her own again. "Oh, Tom," she said. Her anger was growing. "Oh,

Tom," she said. "You should know better. Down there. You know . . ."

Father interrupted, diplomatically. "No, Tom," he said. "Surely you know. Mrs. Jeffry doesn't like us to have ice," and Mrs. Jeffry was keening quietly to herself, looking in at her own folded arms, rubbing her bare elbows free of skin. "Oh, Tom," said Mother, quietly, and she walked around the table and smacked me, quite hard, across the face. It didn't hurt, of course; but, I suppose it helped me to wake up.

It wasn't intensive care. No machines hummed discreetly; no screens pulsed. There was a robust little locker, of sponged wood, and some flowers; there was Sally, of course; it was a cheerful little corner in the cottage hospital. A nurse said, "Oh, so he's woken up, has he?" and Sally stared at me intensely. I said, "What?"

Sally said, "It's all right," which in some indefinable way it clearly was, and I started thinking again, wondering about the silent water. Completely calm, I was, sliding down through the water's roots like a pebble in the earth, pushing it sideways with the soles of my feet, jamming it hard beneath me, wondering with the stillness of complete fear how fast I was moving, how deep I would go. The sea held me by the ears; its currents were in there; I stood, sinking upright, wondering why I was still, in some sense, conscious.

I felt very sick. "They had to pump you out," Sally said. She was laughing; with relief, I suppose. "You had half the English Channel inside you," she added. A nurse said, "Well. It's a peculiar way to go fishing." My arms felt clamped to my sides, as I went down; my shoulders were rigid; I dropped like a stick. A doctor looked hard into my eyes, shining a sharp little light; I learnt later that there was some fear of brain damage; my heart had stopped, for some seconds. "You're a very lucky man," the doctor said. Mrs. Jeffry smiled at me, with Jenny's face. "You're a very naughty boy, Thomas," she said. "What are you?"

Not all of the ghosts are dead. It seemed to me then that, if

I were haunted, it was by more than the old woman. While she jaunted in the air before me, parting it like curtains onto a stage, Jenny lived her half-life there, too, scintillating in the corners of empty rooms, wishing herself at me on draughts from open doors. For ten years, since my dream in the water, I have been seeing the two faces together; the dead one and the other; the fleshless and the pink, perfectly incarnate, twisted yearningly on the bone; for ten years, I have been trying to tell the difference – and to be rid of them both.

Jenny said, "There. Happy birthday. Did you like your present?"

It was October; I had been out of hospital for six weeks – quite cured. Nevertheless, I had told Sally that I had to see a specialist in London, for a final check-up; my lungs might have been affected by the brine. I don't know why I persisted in these obvious lies. We both knew where I was going; we both knew that it was Jenny who had telephoned, not the hospital; Jenny, re-staking her claim after the accident, whispering, "I've got a surprise for you."

I went there resolved to put an end to it. I couldn't lose sight of her face woven into Mrs. Jeffry's; I couldn't lose the sense of evil. I went, as ordered, on the night of my birthday, to say that my life was to be my own, from now on; I felt oddly confident, strangely proud of my second walk down the pier; it was, in a way, an act of bravery. It seemed so simple, as I stood at her door. Both she and the old woman were expressions of my own weakness; I felt that that was behind me, now. A simple act of decision would free me for ever. I was exhilarated.

Jenny opened the door. Her long hair was piled elaborately on top of her head. She was almost completely naked, though her body glistened; it was covered with baby oil. Her mouth was just open, and she was panting gently. What she wore was around her neck: a leather collar, set with jewels of some sort and, hanging from it, a dog's lead.

Later on, I lit a cigarette, and Jenny said, "Good God. You don't still smoke!", but, of course, I did. Jenny had started me, years before; what Jenny started, I continued; so I lay in bed, defeated, again. Jenny giggled, and said, "Remember Toby?", but it meant something different, that particular night, and Jenny howled like a tidy little wolf, and we both laughed, and I though of Mrs. Jeffry's death. That was ten years ago; I was twenty-five years old.

Sally said, "Well. I'd like it. I want it, Tom. We're stuck here, let's face it. We've been going to move for ten years. Let's not go through all that, again. We've got plenty of money. I want the gardens, and the kitchen. I don't mind about the rest. I want my lake."

We were standing in front of the air-raid shelter, our backs to the boards, looking down at the pond, flat as a sea-shell in the spring sunshine. There we stood, side-by-side: a perfect square of a marriage: solid, substantial; nearly happy. It is 1985; we've been married for seventeen years; it seems extraordinary – and not at all bad.

I said, "Yes. I know. It's an awful place, anyway," and Sally said, "Oh, yes. Quite. But it seems to fascinate you," looking at the furrowed pink gables, the steep, grey roof. "We're stuck here, as I say. So let's do something about it, for God's sake."

She would decide; I still hadn't learned to make decisions; I still practised in my mind before going into a shop to buy something. At thirty-five, she was still straight, clear; a simple line in my life. At nights she still washed across me, and said, "Good stuff," and went to sleep in her boy's pyjamas. Things were perplexingly the same.

I said, "It's O.K. The lake used to be bigger, anyway," and she laughed.

"Oh," she said. "Yes. I'd forgotten. The 'lake'."

"Yes," I said. We sat down together; the bench was still there. "No. I don't mean when I was a kid. Mrs. Golley told me. They filled it in, at some point. Before my time." It was true: there had been a lake; though not the lake of my childhood, the awful moonlit ride. "I don't mind putting it back. It's your house, too. I don't mind."

There was no petulance; we were happy, Sally curled in my arm, her shoulder under mine. It was one of the few sunny days we had that spring; we were to have the gardens landscaped; I had painted an awful picture of what they might look like. Sally wanted a lake, stretching past the back lawn, with a rowing-boat, an island in the centre; she wanted a water garden; she would do a lot of it herself. "I don't mind," I said.

"It's a mess, anyway," she said. "Isn't it?" Where the lake would be was the pond, and the shelter, and a huge pile of debris – slot-machines, a toffee-apple hut: the remains of the pier. "That lot," she said, "has got to go."

It had been there ten years. I used to wander down and look at it, for some reason; I climbed on it; once, I pulled out a glass bowl, and smashed it, and found it full of yielding little skeletons, as well as tin rings and plastic spaceships. Another time, I had climbed right to the top – it was about twenty feet high; there, on the ragged summit, were the remains of the toffee-apple kiosk which Bright, intending some sort of favour, had delivered to us from the sea-bed itself. "ICE", it said, bewilderingly, in blemished enamel.

"Yes," I said. "All right. You're right. It's got to go."

In the evening, in the kitchen, we went over the plans. Sally laughed at my painting. "Yes," she said. "Well. It doesn't get a lot better, does it?" and I said, "This is my primitive period," and she said, "Oh, yes. I know. But how long is it going to last?" and I hit her, so that we could laugh. Later, I said, inadvertently, "Would it be safe, though? Seriously? All that water?"

She said, "Safe? What do you mean?"

I said, "Well. You know . . ." though I was regretting it already. The laugh went out of the air; I remembered my father, at the same table, grave about babies. Sally said, "I can't see the point in all that again. You know how it is, about that. You haven't got a leg to stand on."

There we were: almost happy; the house emptying itself of light, yawning away into the night air. "All right," I said.

"It's up to you," she said. "Always has been. You know

where I draw the line." We had no children; Sally refused; it was her one tangible reaction to my visits to London. The lies had finally gone – no more meetings or lung specialists; with her extraordinary clarity of perception, she was prepared to let it go at that. I think that she could see how much I disliked Jenny, how much I despised myself: I think that she could see that was punishment enough. Every few months, I was up there; at thirty-seven, Jenny had lost nothing at all; her abilities were still exquisite; they still are now. I had tried everything; I had even tried to persuade Jenny to give me up. "I think my wife suspects," I'd lied, hoping that she could be frightened off by some sort of court case; I wasn't her only benefactor, by any means. I hadn't told her that Sally knew all about it; it was too humiliating; but I suppose she guessed, anyway. "Never mind," she'd said: "Remember Toby." That was just a few weeks ago.

In any case, there would be no children, while there was Jenny. It was a sacrifice, for Sally; I could see that; she would have been a good mother. But she said that a family needed focus and centre; Jenny took that away. So, as she said, it was up to me.

I suppose that some men would consider Sally the perfect wife, tolerating a mistress, almost without recrimination, for more than fifteen years. I can only say that her straight, linear decency gnawed at me, every day, as I worked my way slowly along the avenue of treachery, shaking and giggling and pleading in Jenny's flat. I can say this now only because, at last, I sense a way out. I stand now, at the end of this story, before what seems to me, quite irrationally, an opportunity to be rid of her. But, then again, I have been wrong before.

In the kitchen, Sally laughed. "Don't worry," she said. "If you fall in, I can always give you the kiss of life."

I remembered coming home from hospital, and saying, "Now. Come on. I'm not in the slightest degree of shock. I want to know what happened."

Sally was lighting a fire; Joyce was pouring out tea; they wouldn't give me any wine. Sally said, "I've told you. It's simple. The jack-thing gave way. Apparently. I don't know. I was watching you. Anyway, the whole lot just cracked open, and down you went.

"Bright was there. He just screamed, like a cat, and stared at me. I thought, well, here we go; I was taking my sweater off, when Bright yells: There! He was looking down, at the beach. Huge bloke, tearing at his clothes, moving like lightning. By the time I'd got down to the water, he was already dragging you out. It seemed like seconds, but actually I think you were in there for quite a bit."

"Oh," I said. "I see." I asked her if she knew who it was, but she didn't; just a spectator. I said, "What about the old woman, then? Do you believe me now?" and Sally said, honestly enough, "I don't know. Do I? All right. There was no body. In the water, I mean. Could have drifted, apparently; but it's not very likely. Granted. And I don't happen to think you're bonkers."

Joyce said, "Oh, no. He's not bonkers. Even when he's being bonkers, as it were," and there was some nervous laughter. A couple of years later, she said to me, "I've always had a lot of time for you, Tom. You know that. I've defended you, as a kid. Perhaps you don't remember. But there's something I want to know."

We were in a boat, oddly enough. Joyce had wanted a trip in a pleasure boat; she lived away from the sea; Sally was elsewhere. We were chugging in a quite unchallenging manner across the little bay. It was off-season; we were virtually alone; a man with a waxy moustache and a blue cap was driving.

"Go on," I said.

"Well," said Joyce. "You must know. I mean. Why? Why do you bother with Jenny? When you've got Sally? Why?"

I didn't see how I could tell her that her daughter had twisted her entire life into an erotic strategy; that the shape of her neck or the pull of her foot would stand stark in my memory for a fortnight. The town opposite ours was called Penmarch; we were meandering towards it, the engine shuddering, the waves knocking us slightly sideways. I said, "What am I supposed to say, Joyce? I mean. If you know about it. I'm sorry. I don't mean . . ."

Joyce said, sadly, "Oh, Tom. It's not Jenny I'm worried about. You can do what you like to her. She's been doing it herself, to everyone else. Since she was about six. Sally's the one I'm thinking of."

I watched the sea; I watched Penmarch, shivering nearer; I watched the man in the little cabin. "Me, too," I said. Weeks later, I was in London again, looking at that face, the eyes, thinking of Mrs. Jeffry, whom I hadn't actually seen or heard from since I fell off the pier. "You are my ghost," I said to Jenny. "You haunt me. You are a patch of cold air in a disused cloakroom."

She giggled. "That's how you think," she said. "I knew you had thoughts like that. You never speak them. You never speak like that. Hardly ever. Your mind is full of these thoughts. But you speak like a dictionary."

I was surprised – because she was so right. In thinking of her as a whore, I had forgotten that she had known me almost as long as anybody; that I had once thought her my greatest friend. "It's all in there, isn't it?" she said, tapping my temple. "But I think it only really comes out when you come to see me, doesn't it?" She lay back, on the bed; she was wearing a gold, silk nightdress and high-heel shoes. "Mmm," she said. "I like being your ghost. Tell me some more."

21

Sally said, "You know what I feel guilty about? Sometimes?" We were watching a J.C.B. gouging a lake into the wasteland. I said, "Sorry? What?"

"When you fell in the water," she said. "The chap who got you out. I was so – you know. Preoccupied, with you. I barely spoke to him. There was the ambulance to get, and everything. I never thanked him. By the time I thought of it, he'd disappeared."

It was a muddy business: the water from the pond seeped through into the new hole; the machine gargled about in it, its tyres sucking into the earth. "What was he like?" I asked. It had occurred to me that it was odd that he should be a stranger.

"Oh. I don't know," she said. "It was a long time ago. Dark, too. Darkish." The digger swivelled and bucked; the mud dripped from its mouth. "He was a good-looking bloke," said Sally. "Broad bloke. I don't know."

I did. I hadn't really thought about it, before; I had realised that he must have been some swimmer; but, standing there with the big house on one side, the sea on the other, I realised that I knew; in some way, I'd known all along. "Did you speak to him?" I asked. "Was he Irish?"

I'd assumed that he'd gone back home; perhaps I'd been wrong. I imagine him travelling about a good deal, comfortably picking up what he can. Perhaps curiosity had drawn him to the beach that afternoon, to see his dead mother's property demolished; I don't know. It had been him, all right; I felt sure of it then, as I glanced down to the empty lodge house; I feel sure of it now. He had cut his way through the sea, shoving it out of his way, romping as he did in the banter of the cross-currents; he had sliced me out of it, the arm on the neck and, dropping me on the beach, he had made some sort of amends – deliberately, or not.

Sally said, "What? Irish? What do you mean?" but she was used to the tight, odd corners in my conversation. I smiled. "It's all right," I said. "Look at that!"

The digger was ramming the pier debris into the back of a lorry. Everything cracked and buckled as the machine fingered it – as the pier itself had done, years before. "Good," said Sally. "That's that," and we sauntered down the little mound, into the kitchen, for lunch.

I don't think that I am merely deluded by hindsight when I say that a weight seemed to be lifting, that morning; the air was growing thinner. Sally made us a salad; we sat together in the square sunshine, listening to the lorry and the generator outside. It was about time for a change; I knew that. Sally used to say, "You just don't change, at all." At one time it had been a compliment; at thirty-five, still nervous of shopkeepers, still talking in the stilted rhythms of a schoolboy, it had become an absurdity. And, of course, if we were ever to have children, it would have to be soon.

"That was O'Cleary," I said. "Who rescued me. He's bowed out."

She didn't understand; neither did I, entirely; but I felt better about him. It is, after all, a fair apology, to save someone's life; even, perhaps, to risk your own. I wondered if he even knew it was me. It didn't seem to matter.

Now that I understand about the ghost, I seem in a way to understand it all. I mean that I seem to understand that it was not knowing that set me apart. I am not, as I have said, of a particularly religious or mystical nature. I've been prepared to accept the possibility of the haunting, there being no decent reason I can see to object to it, the sky rammed full of souls, writhing like jelly-fish. On the other hand, nothing that has happened to me has been conclusive. That is what Sally says, when we talk about it, which, in fact, we don't very often.

Every apparition, every message could have been imagined; the warnings could have been coincidences; I have, after all, had two nervous breakdowns.

Now, I think, I know what it has all been about; it is that that gives me the hope that, this time, I will take control: the deadly distraction of doubt has dissipated, after all these years. In some obscure way, it was starting that lunchtime, a few days ago, when I realised that O'Cleary had grabbed me back – from his mother, so to speak. But that isn't the last episode in this story; nor is it the reason for my optimism. There is one more tale to tell.

It was the afternoon of the same day, early in the spring, in 1985. I don't have a job; I suppose that it's just as well. I have the money; I have the income of the money; I try to look after the houses, and the chip shop, and the Bermuda Guest House. I don't even have a degree in Latin; I gave that up, when I inherited; giving up comes easily. So, that afternoon, I was at home, as usual. I was trying to do a bit of painting, fixing a few men with moustaches onto a Mediterranean kind of lawn, with water behind. It was some sort of picnic.

I was up there, in the room I called the studio, when the machines stopped. The digger restrained itself; I could hear it pulling away, sidling into thought; after two or three weeks, I was an expert on them all. There was a bit of shouting; I didn't think much about it; it was simply a relief when they stopped, the air shuddering into quiet, the silence arching across the garden, settling on the window.

I don't paint pictures any more. I can't do it; I never could. It started when I wandered into the National Gallery, and saw that the arcane lives of spirits and ghosts had been squeezed onto flat surfaces, boxed round, hung up. It seemed an easy way out, somehow; but I knew that I was wrong to try it. The men with moustaches wore bowler hats; they stood like bookends in their spats; they were no use to me. Sally came in and said, "He wants to see you. Mr. Gee. Some problem. I don't know."

* * *

Mr. Gee was the man in charge of the landscaping. He was an old man, in fact; he did little of the fetching and shovelling; three or four lads worked for him. He liked working up there; he said that he knew the house; he was pleased to be cracking the ground open, to be running a lake into it. If I let him, he would discuss the details of it all at length. "You could have some topiary stuff, along there," he would say. "Stick a colonnade next to it. You'll be glad you did."

He was in the kitchen. "Sorry, Mr. Fellows," he said. "Only we wondered what you wanted us to do with this." It was a fine afternoon; the sun was shining, and Mr. Gee said, "Come and have a look," and we walked purposefully across the back lawn, towards the digger, which had been starting work on the old air-raid shelter. Gee said, "Only it seems a shame to pull the thing down. I mean, it's in the way, all right. It's in the way. Of the lake. But it seems a shame . . ."

He took me up the little mound; the bucket of the digger sat gently beside it, waiting to swing against it and knock it out. I said, as we went, "No, Mr. Gee. I'm not particularly interested in preserving an old air-raid shelter . . ." and he said, "No. No . . . What? Shelter? No . . ."

It had been an ornate, brick arch; pretty, indeed, for such an unpleasant function. At some point, the space had been filled with different, modern bricks – for reasons, presumably, of safety. I had sat in front of it, many times, looking at the water below; once, Joyce had told me about lies, in some way, sitting there beside me, and I had seen the beauty in her way of seeing the world – as a sad, delirious fantasy. Some of the men had pulled at the bricks, now; they had opened out the entrance; they were about to bulldoze the lot. I stood beside Mr. Gee; he said, "Yes. Go on. Have a look."

I couldn't see the point. I'd looked into shelters before; there are a number of them surviving around that part of the coast. But Mr. Gee knew what he was at, for all his exaggerated enthusiasm; so I stepped up to the hole in the brick and, cupping my hand on my eye to exclude the light, I looked inside.

It was an egg; about twenty feet deep. My eyes had to work

at the darkness; I had to wait, wondering why old Mr. Gee was wasting my time; then, the egg was there informing the blank pod of the little hillside, growing from black to white in the dusty pockets of my eyes.

I said, "Oh. Christ." Mr. Gee said, "Yes." It was white, inside; the mound held the top third, but the rest was sunk into the land itself: a great, singular bubble.

"Well," said Gee. "What do you think?" I couldn't stop looking; I was leaning in, my chest hurting on the jaw of broken brick; I was craning at it. I said, "Pardon?" and Gee said, "What do you think?"

I spoke back at him, through the cranny; my voice lobbed itself down into the cavity, bounding the tight echo of the cold walls. "I've seen this before," I said.

A few minutes later, I was climbing alone down Gee's ladder, wading into the captive air. The ladder was stable; there was a hook for it, near the entrance; but the deeper I went, the dizzier I felt. It was the bricks; they were set in circle after circle, a solid, dry kaleidoscope, a static whorl, above and below; a tiny, granite whirlwind. It was, as I say, about twenty feet deep; a hundred or more it must have seemed, once, to a small child, set down there, innocently enough, for a photograph, the primitive flash-gun exploding in the entrance above. The ladder wasn't long enough; I dropped the last couple of yards, landing on a straight metal grille, which was the only floor. Landing, I tripped; for a moment, there I was, sitting where she had sat, eighty years before, exactly at the heart.

Gee had gone; a nurseryman had arrived with a van-load of plants. I could hear them talking; the voices crawled in through the entrance, high above me, and then wound around the spiral walls, dipping slowly down through the egg, evolving themselves into slow echoes, pacing the gradual light. The thing had been concealed for nearly a century; I sat there in its inverted dawn as the trapped air shrugged and stretched and the sunshine began to burrow, the shape inflating in the quiet, spring afternoon. There was no dampness; the whitewashed bricks were perfectly dry, stacked infinitely in impossible curves. Sitting down there, at the forgotten base, I steadied myself against the wall, the white settling like dust on my fingers.

I was shivering. A few yards away, the sun was working kindly on the grass; further still, some early trippers were enjoying the empty beach, the sand warming nicely, the gulls showing themselves, perfectly white against the cliffs. I was freezing cold; the new sunlight stood solid, in a discreet shaft, emitting no warmth at all. And, of course, I was nervous; it seemed very possible, then, that the single, tiny entrance could be filled up once more, the light plugged out, the landscape reduced to a small, black hollow for another hundred years.

But it wasn't the cold that made me shake, my thighs gently weak, crouching down there in the silence – Mr. Gee had gone. Nor was it my own fear, nor even the shock of sitting at the centre of a dream, of finding in the corner of a garden the elusive, spinning notion of a dozen fitful mornings. Jenny had called it a Freudian symbol; she'd thought, as she always did, that it proved my passion for her. Once, a frightened schoolboy with a torch, I'd thought I'd seen it; once, Jenny had explained O'Cleary's pathetic deception, hiding the picture to unbalance me further; but I had never, until then, been certain of its reality.

The reason for my shivering was somewhere beside me. I stood up, to get away from it; but the bottom rung of the ladder was well above my head and, for a necessary moment, there was the fleeting thrill of helplessness, the silence growing like the silence in church, sealing the bricks, and the hole, and me. I was standing on a grille, a sort of metal drain-cover, rectangular in shape – the only thing I could see anywhere without curves. In the corner of the grille that was the farthest from me was the fear. It wasn't, of course, my fear; it was hers.

There is no other way to explain it. I could see nothing; there was no noise; I felt that I couldn't even speak, myself. Near my feet was a small, rigid column of terror, located, quite precisely, on the spot where the little girl had sat, listening to someone calling and fussing with a camera. It wasn't just that I could understand the fear; that was easy. I had been frightened myself, even when only looking down into it, peering into the weak, cathedral light. It wasn't just that I assumed the fear of a little girl, who stared upwards, without a smile. It was that it was still there, still as a moth at rest on a wall, fixing the air. It made me shake, though it was nothing to do with me.

There was no distortion of the air, no slight haze, touching the new sunshine in its separate shaft. There wasn't the faintest murmuring, moving sluggishly from the corner, underpinning the gloom. Nothing stirred; no whitewash flaked from the brickwork, reflecting the silent passing of a ghost. There was just a small block of brief terror, intense, but not my own, working away invisibly, spinning without movement, like the egg itself.

It was real, all right. I have been used to confusions between reality and the other thing; I have been accustomed to musty figures, to tweed skirts fluttering between one life and the next. I have seen a foul, old woman spit on the floor, and not known in what sense she could be real; but I was in no doubt, down there, at the bottom of the egg, that someone else's terror was rehearsing itself through me. Well; other people pray, to the sky, and say that it's real. They have no problem with that. A child's fear wore me like a glove, for a few moments. I didn't mind; I knew it wasn't mine. But the shock of it made me shake.

I wasn't trapped, of course. A jump and a scramble would get me onto the ladder, a short pull up the rungs would poke my head back out into the sun; but, nevertheless, I waited a moment or two. It was relief that I was feeling; the relief of finally knowing something, at least, about the egg, and the old woman and, of course, the future. I was sure then, as I am now, that the egg-dreams had come from her. I was sure then, as I am now, that the haunting had been real, all along. And I had the beginning of a notion of what to do about it. Jumping up to the short ladder, I scraped my knees, and grazed my elbows; the whitewash rubbed easily onto my clothes. I must have looked a sight, emerging from the hillside, seconds later, wild-eyed and white. I must have looked like a ghost.

We bought a hot-dog, and went down onto the beach. It was a different beach, since the passing of the pier; it had spread out; some brochures now called it "magnificent"; the old, sordid cosiness had collapsed. "Well," said Sally. "There's your egg, then. Christ." There were still huge concrete stumps, where the pier had stood across the sand. I was leaning on one. "I was never sure," I said. Sally finished her roll, screwed up the paper, threw it into the bin beside my head. "Well," she said. "That's a mystery, all right. I'll give you that."

"No," I said, after a time. Once, I'd been happier – when I was cavorting about the edge of adolescence, with Jenny and O'Cleary, in his old Morris. I'd been happier, but I'd never felt more at peace than I did then. "No," I said. "It's no mystery." She grinned, and frowned; I said, "Come on, Sally. You saw her yourself, once. Come off it."

She said, "Well . . ." Sometimes she said that she just didn't know; sometimes she said that the old lady at the end of the pier had been a trick of the fading light. I didn't want to hear that, then; I said, "There's no mystery. There's just ghosts, that's all. A ghost. Look. Think about it. They put her down that egg thing, to take a picture. She was – what? Five? Four? It's frightening down there. I've been down. You want to go down there. It's all down there. She was terrified. Never forgot it. Those dreams came from her. Where else?"

"I don't know," she said, and I realised that I had never known, myself, exactly what she thought; she'd never really owned up to agreeing with me or thinking me slightly unhinged. "I don't know," she repeated, after a time. "It seems . . . There's something missing, for me. It doesn't all add up."

It did for me. I was lying on the sand, listening to the tiny shouting of some children who were climbing around the caves on the edge of the bay. I was thinking of Mrs. Jeffry, frightened with the entire fear of a child, sunk into a world in which there was only the echo of her own terror for a few, infinite seconds. I was thinking of a whole life devoted to conquering the fear, the photograph by the bed, distorting every relationship. That was the way of her: forcing me into the water, ramming the fear home; pushing me up the tree, spreading before me the photographs of my dead mother. "I've never known such a frightened boy!" she'd said, over and over again, spitting out her own childhood like steam above my head. But the problem had never been solved; I had never grown brave for her, sinking through the dirty ocean, walking the pier to win my first kiss; she had never lost her terror through me.

I realised then that it isn't the ghosts we fear, the prowling monsters, the careful, crawling souls shoving at us through the full air. True or not, the monsters have only the power of myths, or of framed, taut paintings. True fear lies in the corner of any room, the table laid for tea, the well-groomed stranger. Fear lies in the heart of innocence, of pleasure, the taking of a photograph for a faded, forgotten album.

"If she were so frightened," Sally asked, "why keep the picture?"

"Oh," I said. "That was her all over. You don't try to hide from it. You challenge it. Perhaps that's why they moved here – to face up to it. I don't know. Perhaps not. That was how she treated us. Do the things that frighten you."

Sally said, "She sounds awful," and I said, "Oh, yes. You know that. She was." The discovery of the egg had helped me, in some degree, to understand her better; it hadn't made me like her any more than I had before.

The sun dropped out of sight; suddenly, there were only clouds; we left the beach, and walked back up to the egg-entrance. Side by side we stood, peering down into the pit of the hill. "When the sun comes out," I said, "It shines straight down from this hole, like a sort of pillar. The rest of it stays just as dark as it is now. And as cold." Even standing up at the high entrance, we could feel the cold, lifting like mist from the bricks. "It's freezing down there," I said.

After a while, Sally said, "Yes. Well, it would be." The sun had re-emerged; the August shaft stood like a spindle in the darkness. I said, "What? Pardon?"

"It would be freezing, wouldn't it?" said Sally. "I mean, that's what it's meant to be, isn't it?"

I said, "What? Sorry? What do you mean?" and Sally sighed, and said, "Don't you know what this is, Tom?"

It hadn't occurred to me to wonder, up to then. I knew it was an odd shape for an air-raid shelter; I knew that it was the dream that Mrs. Jeffry and I shared; I hadn't thought about it, further. I said. "No. No, I don't. What is it?"

"Well," said Sally. "I think I'm right. We did it at school, I think. I've never actually seen one before. But I don't see how it can be anything else. That's an ice-house."

Mr. Gee was only too pleased to explain. "Oh, yes," he said. "I think old Jeffry had that cleared out. Long time ago. He had plans for it – came to nothing."

I said, "Do you want to come down it?" He seemed interested; I was only trying to be polite, but he said, "Oh, no. No thank you, Mr. Fellows. Rather gives me the willies."

He had some more tea; I offered him a scotch, but he wouldn't; I had one myself, instead. I said, "Well. What about . . . I mean. How did it work?"

"Oh," said Gee. "Oh. Sorry. Thought you knew." He looked at his watch: he loved to talk the afternoons away, solid in the kitchen, while the youths slogged outside. "Well, now," he said. "It's a simple principle. The lake freezes, in the winter. You cut the ice out, cut it into blocks, drop it in there. Keeps it safe, nice and cold, in the summer. A lot of big houses had them, long time ago. Of course, Jeffry had plans for it. Big planner, old Mr. Jeffry. I was a kid then, of course. He set up to sell it, on the pier. An ice stall. For the trippers in the summer. Didn't do much good, though," he added. "I don't think."

I was thinking of my mother's hand, on my face; I was

thinking of a warm little spirit-picnic, Mrs. Jeffry's face when I asked for ice; of the little stack of fear, down at the bottom of the pit, cut and wedged, like a block of ice itself. I said, "What about his wife? Old Mrs. Jeffry?" but Gee knew little about her. "We didn't see much of that one," he said. He looked at his watch again. "Well," he said. "If you'll excuse me." It was five o'clock. Mr. Gee's sociability didn't extend beyond working hours.

I walked out with him. The lads were finishing off, stowing the machines. Much of the so-called lake-bed was now cleared; the ice-house still stood, wrapped in its mound, at one end. The lad had parked the digger beside it. That was to have been the last job, the nudging out of the oval heap, the site for the water-garden, the fountain and the giant lilies. "Well," said Gee. "I hope you'll think about what I've said."

He had spent the afternoon persuading me to leave the thing alone. "After all," he'd said, "there's still plenty of room. For the lake." He was right about that: the bed was carved out, like a lunar sea, the size of a small field; the ice-house was moored, as it were, at one end. "Quite a curiosity," he had said. "What's that buildings museum? Arrowcroft? I'm sure they'd be interested. They number the bricks, you know. Re-build exactly. I could ring them up. If you really want it out of the way."

Sally had joined in. "Come on, Tom," she said. "Air-raid shelter was one thing. This is another. It's got to stay. It's obvious."

She couldn't understand it. I'd been sentimental enough over the pier, ten years before; she couldn't see why I seemed to be contemplating knocking down what Mr. Gee called "a real lump of heritage". We were sitting, the three of us, on the back lawn, in the middle of the afternoon; I said, "Yes. Well. Let's see." I could hear Mrs. Jeffry; she was, perhaps, just inside the kitchen door, or just beyond the hedge; the voice was fervent, but indistinct. "Have some more tea," I said to Gee, and Sally said, "We could even use it. You never know. Make our own ice. I bet the lake will freeze. In the winter." She was seeing it already, the water solid and massive, heaving at the banks. Gee had some more tea; he liked a lot of sugar; the diggers juddered and swivelled, just out of sight. "Well, of course," he said. "It's up to you, Mr. Fellows. If you don't want it. What you say, goes," and I said, absently, "Yes, that's right," and Sally looked very black, indeed. At five o'clock, Gee said, "I hope you'll think about what I said," and Sally said, "Oh, yes. We will."

Later on, she said, "You were rude to him. I can't understand it. You're never rude." She was right; for all my faults, I have never liked to upset people. I said, "Do you remember my dream? About the ice?" We were in bed; the argument was there too, fretting about between us, making room for itself where it could.

Sally said, "What?" and I said, "In hospital that time." She was quiet; I thought she was asleep; but after a while, she said, "Tell me," so we were both, for a minute or two, drinking dead lemons on a summer lawn. She thought about it, and then she sighed; I could feel the warmth of her, all down one side of me. She said, "You live in dreams. You know that?" She wasn't angry, or sarcastic; the words found a measure in the darkness. "Other people come out of their dreams in the daytime. You seem to do the opposite."

I thought about that, as I listened to her falling asleep. I saw myself crawling, dishevelled and wrong-headed, from the recess of the dream onto the soft bank of evening. It was like mining; if you were lucky, you came up with a nugget of truth.

It's difficult to wake Sally. Already, she was asleep, the body folded tidily, unneeded before morning. Nevertheless, I crept to the window with a kind of courteous stealth. The moonlight was yellow; I could see the lake-bed, dry and rutted after the hard afternoon sunshine; the tractor and the digger stood like ghosts, frozen in forgotten attitudes, like a couple of museum dinosaurs.

I keep a chair, by the window, because not sleeping is normal with me. I sit there more often than not, keeping an odd, disjointed vigil, checking the snow, or the wind, or the drift of constellations. That night, I was looking down at a thin, timid boy walking on the echo of a garden pond; farther off were an old woman, scolding beside a compost-heap, a lad chucking broken crab-apples, a pretty, flirting young girl in a white dress. I saw them all, in my mind; I saw a big, glinting Irishman, playing tennis, the racquets knocking about in the air. The mound of the ice-house stood, perfectly solid, a great bee-hive in the amber moonlight. "You're the scaredest boy I know," said the old woman; but I wasn't, after all, as scared as her.

After a while, I was going downstairs, wearing shoes, not slippers, sending slight footfalls into the wood. Nobody lives here, beside us; Sally despises the notion that she needs help in looking after me; so there was no need to creep, across the hallway, into the kitchen, collecting the keys which Mr. Gee left with us every night, so that he couldn't forget them. Relaxed enough, I felt, unlocking the back door, glancing back at the rowans, craning in the orange light. The crab and the willow stood flat on the back lawn; all the shadows had gone. Darkness sat in my lungs; the spring night was sharp on my lips. "Here you are, then," I said.

I had some idea of how to do it; I had watched them, often enough, wondering stupidly about painting a picture of it. "Here you are, then," I said again, as I tried to climb up into the digger, my foot trying three different places, the seat suddenly high above me. It was hard, when I reached it, but oddly comfortable, rounded like a barrel against my back.

I think that Mrs. Jeffry was on at me; I could feel the voice working like a fist, clenching and unclenching at the back of my neck; but I couldn't hear what she was saying. "It's all right," I said, because at that moment I understood the will – her will, in fact, in more ways than one. "It's got to stay," Sally had said; I thought of that as I shook the ignition key into the unfamiliar lock. There was Jenny, grinning, her teeth like tiny ripples, her nose a skeleton's nose, her skin the dry sketch of a childhood fancy. "You can't help it," she seemed to say: it was all she ever said; and Mrs. Jeffry said, "Come on now, Thomas, boy. Where there's a will, there's a way."

I looked up to see Sally at the bedroom window and I realised that the machine had started, the noise was generating itself out from somewhere below. There was a whole row of levers, in front of me; the one in the middle made it go; the others worked the buckets, in some way. I looked up, again, and the face was gone; she was on her way down; I knew what she would do, so I threw the middle lever forward, and was suddenly terrified as the whole thing jolted off, like a statue waking up, lumbering, the giant wheels planting themselves like feet.

The night shook with the row of it, though I felt oddly detached, perched up there in the pinnacle, the bucket lunging around in the empty air as I wrenched the levers. "Right," I said, eventually, and began. As I did so, Sally appeared at the back door and immediately began running. The bucket heaved on the arm, the great elbow slapped itself straight, the hydraulics sang. She would try to stand between me and the ice-house, I knew that; she thought that I was temporarily deranged, that we could talk it over in the morning. I pulled a lever backwards; they had huge, smooth spheres on, for handles; I wrenched with both hands, so the bucket careered upwards, its teeth opening, drooling mud from the afternoon. Sally was beside me, down to the left; she yelled, "All right! All right! Get down!" and another lever sent the tub of a bucket off to the side. "Look out!" I yelled; the whole front arm of the thing was shifting towards her; I had little idea of how it worked. The seat I was on rocked; the body seemed unstable, as the one huge limb whipped around me. "Look out!" I shouted. The bucket hit the ground; I felt the entire machine begin to rise, stretching, bracing itself against the earth, shoving itself upwards like a circus elephant. Sally shouted, "All right! For God's sake, get down!" but I couldn't have, even if I'd wanted to. She moved in front of me, then; she ran beneath the hydraulic arm, under the crooked archway; she was trying to find a way up to me. I knew then, with complete clarity, that I had only to demolish the thing. That was why I was there. A couple of decent bashes and the whole lot would crumble like fudge and she would begin to leave me alone. They both would.

Sally was beside me as I did it. She was screaming; I wasn't listening. I began, briefly, to enjoy it; I began to see how it worked; I took the ice-house down in three, hefty sweeps, and then I patted it on top, flattening it down like a pastry-cook. Sally was sobbing when I turned off the engine; the sound was suddenly the only sound, the garden was alone with it, with the soft, staccato sobs of a woman. I was panting, myself; it had been hard work.

"There," I said, calmly. I am still as calm, now. "There. She won't bother us again."

After a while, Sally stopped crying, and leant against me. We perched there together, on the single seat of the J.C.B. I said, "Well. What do you think? I think it's romantic," and she chuckled, and breathed in from a long way out, and said, "Oh. Definitely. I think we should get one. You could take me up dark lanes in it," and she laughed out loud, because she knew that something had happened, though she didn't know what.

The ice-house now was a soft concoction of earth, bricks and spent mortar; the digger's bucket was still huddled in a corner of it. There was no secret panic, in there; no discreet wall of circular cadence, no tiny yearning for the light. The yellow moon lay complete over everywhere; the cold belonged to the garden, and the spring; not to the pillared echo of a dead fear.

Sally said, "I'm getting a chill." We climbed down, onto the ground, and looked again at the rubble, which looked like the other heaps of rubble which were all over the garden. "Who?" said Sally.

I said, "What? Who what?" and she said, "Who won't bother us again?" I looked at the two trees, as we walked hand-in-hand across the back lawn: the crab, and the willow; they were both in leaf, tugging the green spindles out of themselves. The crab was compact; the sour apples had the whole summer to wait before they knocked the flowers to the ground; and the willow was turning languid again, the leaves feathering the web into an embrace. "Come on," said Sally. "I think I know. Tell me. Who won't bother us?" and, because for years I hadn't been able to think of them as separate, I said, "Neither of them."

The fields are piled up around the bay, stacked like blankets beneath the wind which works the sea-water in gentle drifts across the beach, the field and the garden. Mr. Gee is laying the water-lilies across our lake. Occasionally, he glances at the space left by the ice-house, and frowns. I think he thinks I was drunk.

I watched him this morning, for a time; then I wandered up onto the headland, seeing the spring rain joining the land to the sea. The beach was clear. No Morris traveller shunted onto the promenade; no teenage girl stained the white sand with her deft skin. By the hot-dog stand, no ridiculous eight-year-old sidled about, trying to understand.

I don't know, exactly, what I've done. I don't know whether I've committed an act of acquiescence or defiance, smashing up a bit of an old woman's life that she hadn't smashed up for herself, the bit of separate fear that she had tried to face in the garden, in the photograph. What I do know is that Sally is smiling, that Jenny's neck no longer smarts against my shoulder, and that the ghosts have shuffled away.

They haven't ceased to exist, of course. I know that, somewhere or other, they are rammed thickly together; I suppose that, one day, I shall join them. But I do know that they aren't in the garden, or on the Moor, or in the unused bedrooms of the old house. They aren't in the rowan avenue, either; I found it clear this morning, the quick stretch down to the lodge, where nobody lives. I walked down, between the tall trunks, hearing my feet alone on the gravel; I looked into the little house; I had to check it, because it is let for the next two weeks. It is all Mrs. Jeffry's: the bed, the furniture, the television. Even the pictures are still there; every picture but one, of course. I looked, as I always do, out of habit, at the space on the window-sill where the egg-picture should have been; I laughed a little, quietly, thinking of O'Cleary, hiding it away.

At the bottom of a bottom drawer in her dressing-table are some other photographs: the bright, wanly optimistic pictures of my mother which the old woman had somehow appropriated. I found them there, years ago; for some reason, I never got round to moving them away. I spread them out, this morning, and looked for a time at the pretty, vacuous face, caught by the camera in a series of enhanced emotions. After a minute or two, I chose one I particularly liked and, emptying one of Mrs. Jeffry's numerous gilt frames, I framed my mother, instead. I have put the picture on the dresser in the kitchen.

I came back up the rowan path and let the air bob my head, glancing from the sea to the house. About half-way up, near the tree where Jenny had leant and lit and sucked the one cigarette, a sudden blankness stopped me. A swallow was blotting the sun, running and leaping in the small spring sky above me. I watched it for a time, fielding itself in the sharp air, coasting, agile as a cat. It went for the sea, presently, and I climbed up the bank to watch it as it shot and quivered about, cavorting farther and farther away, blinking into a full-stop.

I stayed there, for a few seconds. It was time to come home; we were due to go out, to lunch – a charity lunch, with Doctor Lister. It was time to get changed, and start talking about a heart-lung machine; Sally would be waiting. Nevertheless, I spent just a few morning seconds there, looking at the air.

It wasn't the sand that held me, white though it is; it wasn't the cosy landscape of familiar cliffs. It certainly wasn't the water; I have never understood the attractions of that, the seductive giving-away, the little, suffocating ripples. What took my attention, and holds it still, now, was the clarity of line between me and it. The air didn't shove me; it didn't seem set to shift in ponderous blocks or crumple beside my ear. It didn't seem stiff with warnings; my breath moved through it, easily – as it moved through me. Walking back to the house, I noticed that the rowans were flowering. They have many thousands of tiny, white flowers – unromantic, like cauliflower heads; it seemed to me this morning that I could have counted each one, the light working separately at them. But, oddly enough, it is the air above the sea I remember; a picture so familiar and yet, this morning, the first empty landscape of my adult life.